THEODORE BOONE
THE ACCOMPLICE

READ ALL OF THEODORE BOONE'S ADVENTURES!

Theodore Boone: Kid Lawyer

Theodore Boone: The Abduction

Theodore Boone: The Accused

Theodore Boone: The Activist

Theodore Boone: The Fugitive

Theodore Boone: The Scandal

JOHN GRISHAM

THEODORE BOONE
THE ACCOMPLICE

PUFFIN BOOKS

PUFFIN BOOKS
An imprint of Penguin Random House LLC, New York

First published in the United States of America by Dutton Children's Books,
an imprint of Penguin Random House LLC, 2019
Published by Puffin Books, an imprint of Penguin Random House LLC, 2020

Visit us online at penguinrandomhouse.com

THE LIBRARY OF CONGRESS HAS CATALOGED THE DUTTON CHILDREN'S BOOKS EDITION AS FOLLOWS:
Names: Grisham, John, author.
Title: Theodore Boone : the accomplice / by John Grisham.
Description: New York : Dutton Books for Young Readers, [2019] | Series: Theodore Boone ; [7] | Summary: "When his best friend Woody is arrested—an unwitting accomplice to a robbery—Theodore Boone must work to prove his innocence"—Provided by publisher.
Identifiers: LCCN 2019012587 (print) | LCCN 2019016766 (ebook) |
ISBN 9780525556275 (ebook) | ISBN 9780525556268 (hardback)
Subjects: | CYAC: Lawyers—Fiction. | Family problems—Fiction. | Robbers and outlaws—Fiction. | Middle schools—Fiction. | Schools—Fiction. | BISAC: JUVENILE FICTION / Law & Crime. | JUVENILE FICTION / Mysteries & Detective Stories. |
JUVENILE FICTION / Action & Adventure / General.
Classification: LCC PZ7.G88788 (ebook) | LCC PZ7.G88788 Thcr 2019 (print) | DDC [Fic]—dc23
LC record available at https://lccn.loc.gov/2019012587

Puffin Books ISBN 9780525556282

Text set in Minion Pro

Printed in the United States of America

1 3 5 7 9 10 8 6 4 2

To Margot Renée Linden.
Welcome.

THEODORE BOONE
THE ACCOMPLICE

CHAPTER 1

Boy Scout Troop 1440 was dismissed by Major Ludwig promptly at five p.m. on Tuesday afternoon, and the boys hustled outside to their bikes. As always, Theodore Boone lingered for a moment to say good-bye to the Major, then he stepped into the cool evening with plans to head downtown to his parents' law firm.

At the bike rack he saw Woody Lambert, one of his good friends, and noticed once again that he wasn't smiling. Woody never smiled these days, and that in itself would not have been noticeable except that in place of a smile or a grin or any sign that life was normal or even okay, Woody was going about his business with a sad, sour expression, as if life was beating him up. As if he carried burdens and problems too heavy for a thirteen-year-old boy.

Theo had known him since the fourth grade when the Lamberts moved to Strattenburg. Their home was unstable. His mother was on her second or third husband, and the current one was often away on the job. His real father had disappeared years ago. His older brother Tony had been arrested once and was gaining a bad reputation. Theo suspected that the Lamberts were having serious problems and that was why Woody seemed so unhappy.

Theo said, "Let's go to Guff's and get a frozen yogurt. My treat."

Woody immediately shook his head no, even frowned. "No thanks."

He never had spare change, and he was too proud to allow Theo or anyone else to treat. Theo had known this for a long time and felt like a jerk for offering to pay.

"You okay?" Theo asked.

"I'm fine," Woody said as he climbed on his bike. "See ya later."

"Call me if you need me," Theo said, and watched him ride away. Woody did not respond.

Home was the last place Woody wanted to go, though he suspected the house would be empty. His mother was working two part-time jobs and on Tuesdays she waited tables at a diner near the college. Her husband, Woody's stepfather, worked in construction and made good money at times, but the jobs were sporadic. Currently he was out of town, two hours away, and Woody hadn't seen him in a month. Tony was a sophomore at Strattenburg High but was in the process of dropping out, or flunking out, or getting kicked out for bad grades and low attendance. Tony's attitude was so lousy he didn't care how he left the school.

Woody parked his bike under the carport, walked through the unlocked door to the kitchen, yelled for Tony, heard nothing, and was pleased no one was there. He was spending a lot of time alone, and it wasn't all that bad. He had choices, options. He could play video games, watch television, do his homework, or plug in his electric guitar and practice for an hour or so. Of the four, homework, of course, ranked last. His grades were slipping and his teachers were asking questions, but no one at home seemed to care.

There was rarely anyone at home.

Theo parked his bike outside the rear door of Boone & Boone, the converted old house his parents had owned since long before he was born. He entered through the door, stepped into his own little office, and was immediately met by Judge, his faithful dog who'd been waiting for hours. Judge spent his days at the office doing nothing of any importance except sleeping and begging for food. He moved quietly around the place, napping on one small dog pallet for an hour or so before easing along to another. He had at least four beds, three downstairs and one up, but his favorite was the soft one located under Theo's desk. Each afternoon, in anticipation of his best friend returning from school, Judge went to Theo's office and waited.

Theo rubbed his head, chatted with him for a moment, then the two of them went to say hello. Vince, the paralegal, had left for the day and his door was closed. Dorothy, the real estate secretary, was hard at work but stopped for a second to inquire as to how Theo's day had gone. The door to his mother's large office was closed, a clear indication that she was meeting with a client. She was a divorce lawyer, most of her clients were women, and when they met behind closed doors things were usually tense. Theo did not even think about knocking.

He had no plans to be a divorce lawyer. At the age of thirteen, he had already decided that he would become either a great courtroom lawyer, the best in the state with big, important trials, or a great judge who presided over those trials and was known for his wisdom and fairness. Most of his friends were dreaming of careers as professional athletes, or computer geniuses, or brain surgeons, or perhaps even a rock star or two, but not Theo. He loved the law and longed for the day when he was a fully grown man with dark suits and a fine leather briefcase. However, according to his parents, he must first finish the eighth grade, then suffer through high school, college, and law school. At least twelve more years of education awaited him, and he was not looking forward to the ordeal. At times he was already tired.

The front room of Boone & Boone was ruled by Elsa Miller, the firm's long-time receptionist/secretary/paralegal/adviser/referee, and, occasionally in the past, Theo's babysitter. Elsa did it all, and she did it with an enthusiasm that Theo often found tiresome.

At the sight of him, she bounced up from her desk, grabbed him, hugged him, pinched both cheeks, all the while asking how his day had gone. It was the daily routine and it rarely changed.

"Just another boring day in school," Theo said as he tried to wiggle out of her embrace.

"You always say that. How was Scouts?"

Elsa knew his schedule better than he did. If he had an appointment with the doctor or dentist, Elsa had it marked on her calendar. A science project due? Elsa reminded him. A scouting trip to the lake? Elsa was on it.

She looked him up and down to make sure his shirt

matched his pants, another irksome habit, and said, "Your mother is with a client but your father is free right now."

His father was always free, and alone. Woods Boone was a real estate lawyer who smoked a pipe, and because of the smoke no one else in the firm ventured upstairs near his office.

"Better hop on your homework," Elsa said as she retreated to her desk.

Every school day of his life at least three people—his parents and Elsa—reminded him to do his homework. And the irritating part of it was that Theo always did his homework. No one had to remind him. Not once in his student life had he failed to do his homework, yet he was constantly being reminded to get it done.

At times he wanted to snap at them, all three of them, but that would cause more trouble than it was worth. And it wouldn't help matters. Part of being a good kid was learning to overlook the shortcomings of adults. They liked to repeat things, especially his father, and especially those little commands that were supposed to make Theo a better person. Brush your teeth. Comb your hair. Eat your vegetables. Ride carefully and watch for traffic. Do your homework. The list seemed endless.

So instead of arguing, he said "Yes, ma'am," and walked to the stairs. Judge was at his heels and they headed up, making as much noise as possible. His father was known to nap in the late afternoon and Theo, being a good kid, did not want to embarrass him by barging in mid-snore.

But Mr. Boone was wide awake and lost in the usual pile of papers on his desk. A thick, rich aroma of pipe smoke hung in the air, which Theo had never found to be unpleasant.

"Well, hello, Theo," his father said, looking up as if surprised, the same greeting virtually every afternoon.

"Hey, Pop," Theo said as he fell into a soft leather chair across the desk. "Are you busy?"

"Busy?" Mr. Boone repeated as he waved his arms at the mountain of paperwork, as if he had far too many clients. "Never too busy for you. How was school?"

"Boring as always, but Scouts was fun. We're headed to the lake in two weeks."

"I know. The Major invited me to tag along, but not this time."

They'd had this conversation at least three times already. "Dad, I'm worried about something."

"Let's hear it."

"It's Woody. He's acting strange, like he's worried all the time. His grades are not good, and the teachers are watching him pretty close."

"Trouble at home, you think?"

"Probably. His big brother Tony is hanging out with some bad kids, skipping school, staying out late, stuff like that, and he has a lot of influence over Woody. Their mom works a couple of part-time jobs and is not home much. His stepfather works out of town and Woody doesn't like the guy anyway. We're going camping in two weeks and Woody says he's not going, says he needs to do some yard work around the house. The truth is that he probably doesn't have the money to make the trip. He's always broke these days. I'm really worried about him."

"Does he have many friends?"

"You know Woody, Dad. He's a popular guy who gets a lot of respect because he's the toughest kid in class. If there's a fight, Woody either starts it or finishes it or breaks it up. Nobody messes with him, and he sort of likes his tough-guy role. It looks like Woody is headed down the wrong road, at least in my opinion. I wish there was some way we could help him."

"You can be his friend and talk to him, Theo. He's always liked you. Be a positive influence. Encourage him to study and do his homework. Talk about what it will be like when you guys go off to high school next year. The sports, the girls, the football games, the field trips, all the fun stuff you'll be involved in."

"I guess. I don't suppose there's anything you and Mom could do."

"I'll talk to her and we'll think about it, but it's usually a bad idea to get involved with somebody else's kid. We've got our hands full raising you." He laughed, but Theo wasn't in the mood for humor.

"Thanks, Dad. I'd better get busy with the homework."

"Sure, Theo. And I'll discuss it with your mother."

Theo and Judge went downstairs to his little office. Judge curled up on his bed and immediately went to sleep, completely unworried about anything. Theo envied him. The life of a dog. Sleeping, eating, occasionally chasing squirrels and rabbits, no troubles at all.

CHAPTER 2

It was after dark when Woody heard the kitchen door slam. He was in the den watching television, bored. Tony bounced in with a big smile and said, “Hey, kid, what’re you doing?”

“Nothing. Where you been?”

“Hanging out. Any word from Mom?”

“No. She works until ten on Tuesdays.”

Tony fell onto the sofa and kicked off his sneakers. “What are you watching?”

“Clint Eastwood. An old western.”

“You watch the weirdest stuff. Have you had dinner?”

“There’s nothing to eat. I’ve already checked.”

"Look, I gotta deliver some pizzas tonight. Why don't you come with me and we'll grab one on the run?"

A pizza sounded like a good idea, though they ate a lot of them. Tony worked a few hours a week delivering for a popular pizza joint called Santo's, and he usually managed to grab a few leftover slices for himself and Woody. Often, he managed to steal an entire supreme.

"All right," Woody said without moving. Tony bounced off the sofa, went to his room, and returned seconds later wearing his red Santo's polo and matching red cap. Woody turned off the television and the lights and they left the house.

Tony drove a small Toyota pickup with a million miles on it, a hand-me-down from their stepfather. It wasn't much of a ride and the girls weren't too impressed with it, but for the time being it was all they had. Ten minutes later they pulled into the parking lot of a strip mall, and Tony parked as far away from Santo's as possible.

"Keep down," he said as he got out.

"I know, I know," Woody said as he slid low in the seat. Santo's had a No-Riders policy and the boss was strict about it. While making deliveries, any driver caught with a passenger would be fired on the spot. Tony disappeared into the restaurant and Woody began the waiting. Peeking out the window, he watched college students spill out of their cars and enter Santo's. Cute girls, cool guys, nice cars. Woody wondered if he would ever make it to college. He was having doubts, though at the age of thirteen he really wasn't too concerned about it. In his gang, only Theo and perhaps one or two others had their futures planned. Woody was leaning toward a career as a fireman, and he wasn't sure if college was necessary.

His phone pinged with a text from his mother. Have you seen Tony? What are you having for dinner?

Woody responded: We R fine. Pizza. You good?

Okay but may work until 11. Okay with that?

Sure.

Homework done?

Of course.

She asked about his homework only because she was expected to. The truth was Daisy was too tired to monitor her sons' progress in school. She knew Tony was skipping a lot because the school called her, and they were fighting about it. But Tony was winning because his mother simply didn't have the energy to keep up with him. Things were not going well with her current husband. She was worrying a lot and losing sleep. Daisy was always tired and frazzled, and Woody was concerned. With her earnings from two part-time jobs, plus what little her husband kicked in, the family was barely staying afloat.

How was Woody supposed to dream of college? It was easy for someone like Theo, with two parents who were lawyers and seemed to be happily married. Plus, Theo was an only child. He had been Woody's loyal friend for many years, and would always be, but at times Woody secretly admitted to himself that he was envious of Theo.

Tony walked out with the bright red magnetic Santo's sign and affixed it to the top of the Toyota. "Should be only a few minutes," he said, and went back inside. Woody said nothing. Ten minutes later, Tony was back with four large pizza boxes, which he placed on the bench seat between them. They smelled delicious and Woody was suddenly starving. When they were on the street, Tony said, "Open the top one and let's have dinner. Sausage and mushrooms."

Woody opened the box, handed a slice to Tony, and took one for himself.

They ate in silence as Tony zipped through narrow streets around the college, driving, as always, much too fast. The first stop was a run-down duplex with cars scattered in the front yard. Tony checked the address, parked in the street, and hustled to the front door with a large pizza. He was back in seconds, and grumbling, "Kid gave me a buck. A twelve-dollar pizza and Mr. Big Spender tipped me only a buck. College kids." They sped away and stopped two blocks over at another student dump. Another one-dollar tip.

But they were having fun, cutting through the maze of streets around Stratten College, listening to loud music on the radio, eating dinner, and griping about how cheap the students were. When the last pizza was delivered, Tony raced back to Santo's for another load. The restaurant was packed and the delivery phone rang nonstop. It was dinnertime and the students were hungry.

They squealed tires and took off again, with a rack of warm pizzas between them. Tuesdays were normally slow, but Santo's was shrewdly offering a two-for-one special and business was brisk. For two hours, Tony and Woody wheeled around the western section of Strattenburg, delivering mostly to students but to some nicer homes as well. When things slowed around nine, Tony had collected twenty-seven dollars in tips and was proud of himself. He gave Woody a five-dollar bill and said he would give his mother a ten. But Woody doubted that.

They stopped for gas at a convenience store on the edge of town. Someone called Tony's name, and a friend named Garth walked over as he left the store. Tony was pumping gas and Woody couldn't hear all of their conversation, but he did hear Garth say, "Let's go cruising. Got some beer and a tank full of gas."

Garth drove a muscled-up green Mustang with wide wheels and loud mufflers, and he was known to speed around town. He wasn't a bad kid, in fact he was quite popular and dated one of the cutest girls Woody had ever seen. But there was something about Garth that Woody didn't like. He had the look of a guy who might break bad at any minute and do something stupid. He was eighteen, a year older than Tony but still too young to buy beer, and the fact that he had some was a bad sign. Tony finished pumping and parked the truck beside the store.

"You going with us?" he asked Woody.

"What am I supposed to do? Walk home?"

"Let's go. We'll just cruise around for a while and get home before Mom."

The smart voice in Woody's head said no. Do not get in the car with Garth and Tony and cruise around the college while drinking beer. Nothing good could happen. And the not-so-smart voice said, Oh, go ahead. It's harmless fun. How many thirteen-year-olds get to hang out with the older guys?

"Are you coming with us?" Tony snapped at him, but it was more than a question. It was a challenge. What Tony was really asking was: Are you gonna chicken out and go home and wait for Mommy?

Woody didn't flinch, didn't hesitate. "I'm coming," he said, and shrugged as if he could run with the big dudes any night of the week. He crawled into the back seat of the

Mustang as Garth gunned the engine. The car roared and fishtailed out of the parking lot.

"Gimme a beer," Garth said over his shoulder as he darted through traffic. Woody saw a six-pack of cans on the seat next to him. He pulled off two and handed them to Tony, who said, "You can have one."

It was another challenge. Garth was watching in the rearview mirror and asked, "How old are you, Woody?"

"Thirteen."

"Ever had a beer?"

"Sure."

"We've had a few together," Tony said. "Sneak them from the fridge when no one's home."

There was one massive, gigantic problem in the car with them. Woody could feel it, almost touch it as if it were seated next to him, and he came very close to simply blurting it out just to clear his conscience. Tony was on probation. Four months earlier he had been arrested for possession of pot, which was bad enough, but he had also been charged with intent to sell. He got an incredibly lucky break when the two narcotics officers who nailed him collapsed. One was fired for stealing drugs. The other fled town and had not been seen. The evidence disappeared along with the policemen, and for a few weeks Tony was the luckiest kid in Strattenburg. He agreed to plead guilty to a lesser charge of underage possession and got off light with six months' probation. He spent only one night in jail and considered the entire episode a joke. It did not faze him, and he continued slipping through the cracks at school.

If he got caught with beer, it would be a violation of his probation and he would likely spend a few nights in the slammer. But Tony wasn't worried about anything these days. He was seventeen, going to school when he pleased and enjoying the life of a future high school dropout.

"I had my first beer when I was ten years old," Garth said proudly. "My crazy uncle gave it to me. He's in prison, you know? Go ahead, Woody, help yourself."

The truth was, Woody had tasted beer a few times, always in an effort to be cool in front of Tony, but he couldn't stand the taste of it. After years of watching beer commercials in which young and beautiful and athletic people lived the good life with a cold beer in hand, he was shocked at how awful it tasted. He had mentioned this to Tony who promised him that with enough practice he would grow to enjoy it.

Garth, still glancing back, said, "Come on, kid, pop a top."

Woody pulled off a beer, popped it, took a sip, and tried to look as if he really enjoyed it, but wanted to spit it out. He managed to choke it down without a frown, then gritted his teeth and took another swallow. Then another. The taste did not improve.

"I think he likes it," Garth said between gulps.

If you only knew, Woody said to himself. Tony and Garth enjoyed their drinks far more than Woody and within minutes were tossing back their empties and demanding more. Woody handed them their seconds and took another sip. He began to get light-headed and this helped with the bad taste. He finally finished his first can and popped the top to his second.

"Attaboy," Garth said without turning around. They turned into a parking lot around a large mall and circled it until they approached a Cineplex.

"There's his car," Tony said, as if he really didn't want to meet whoever owned the car. It was parked with several others, all jacked-up muscle cars, all with tough guys leaning on the fenders and smoking cigarettes. Garth parked close by and turned off his ignition. "Let's get it over with."

"Stay here," Tony said to Woody as he got out.

No problem, Woody thought. He watched Garth and Tony approach the other guys, say hello, shake hands in a variety of ways, and light up their own cigarettes. Nobody was holding a beer or a drink. A police car eased by not far away. The boys waved. The cops waved back. Everybody was behaving.

Woody kept low in the back seat, barely peeking through the window. The boys laughed and bantered back and forth, then the conversation grew serious. Both Garth and Tony reached into their pockets, took out money, and handed it over to a bearded guy who looked a few years older. He gave them nothing in return. Woody doubted that neither his brother nor Garth would be stupid enough to buy pot in such an open area that was patrolled by the police. There were probably cameras everywhere. Still, the transaction, whatever it was, had the look of something shady.

When they returned to the car, Woody asked, "Who was that guy with the beard?"

Garth started the car and began to ease away. Tony said nothing. Woody asked again, "Who was that guy with the beard?"

Tony said, "An old friend." But it was obvious the guy was not an old friend, and Tony just wanted his little brother to shut up. No one spoke for a few minutes as Garth drove along Main Street, going nowhere in particular. Finally, he said, "I need some more beer."

The six-pack was gone. Each had consumed two cans.

"I'm broke. You got any cash left?" Garth asked Tony.

"No. Gave it all to him."

"What?" Woody asked. "How can you be broke? You had over twenty bucks a while ago."

Tony turned around and glared at his little brother. “That guy back there is a friend of ours. He’s a bookie at the college, handles bets on football games. We owed him some money. No big deal. Sometimes you win, sometimes you lose. How about loaning me that five bucks I just gave you?”

“I don’t think so.” Woody wanted to say something about the gambling, which, of course, was also against the law and would be another violation of Tony’s probation.

“Forget it,” Garth said. “We’re not taking money from a kid.”

He braked hard and pulled into a shopping center. All the stores were closed but a well-lit ATM machine was waiting. Garth parked, left the engine running, walked to the machine, looked around nervously as if robbing a bank, and began punching numbers. He punched and punched without success. He stomped away, returned to the car, said, “I guess my mom’s frozen my account again. I really want a beer.”

They sped away with the Mustang burning rubber.

The convenience store was on the edge of town, on a two-lane road with little traffic. The parking lot was gravel and the front windows were covered with thick bars. Two pumps offered gasoline but there were no other customers at that moment.

Garth parked and said, "I know this guy. Be right back."

"What's he doing?" Woody asked, almost in a whisper.

"Don't worry about Garth. He knows everybody."

They waited but not long. Garth soon appeared, making a quick exit and holding an entire case of canned beer. He yanked open his door, tossed the beer into Woody's lap, jumped in, and shifted gears. The Mustang roared away from the store, spraying gravel all over the place.

"Beers please!" Garth said, obviously proud of himself. Woody pulled off two cans and handed them to the front. He was finished for the night.

"How'd you get the beer?" he asked when the store was out of sight.

"Just told the guy I was thirsty, needed to borrow some beer." Garth popped a top and slugged his beer.

"Come on," Tony said. "The guy gives you credit?"

Garth smacked his lips and wiped his mouth with the back of his hand. He reached into his left jeans pocket and pulled out something. It was a black pistol, shiny in the darkness. "This is instant credit all over town," Garth said with a laugh. He turned around quickly, aimed it at Woody's face, and pulled the trigger.

A blast of warm water hit Woody in the eyes. His heart had stopped in a split second and his mouth opened in horror. Garth roared with laughter as he turned his attention back to the highway.

Tony was not amused and yelled, "What are you doing? You robbed that guy?"

"No, of course not," Garth said, still laughing. "You can't rob someone with a water pistol. I just borrowed some beer, and some of his cash, and I'll go back tomorrow and pay the guy."

"You took cash?!" Tony yelled again in disbelief.

Woody was too stunned to think. Water was still dripping into his mouth, and he was in shock from being shot. But he quickly began to realize that the situation was a lot more serious than Garth was letting on.

"You're crazy," Tony said. "You can't stick a gun in a guy's face. I don't care what kind of gun it is."

"It's not a gun. It's a water pistol, and a very nice one at that. Just having a little fun."

"How much cash did you take?"

"Not much. All he had. He emptied the drawer. I'd say a couple of hundred."

"Look, Garth, we're going home," Tony said angrily. "Take us back to my truck. You got that? I'm on probation, remember? A stupid trick like that will bring in the cops and I'm headed to jail. I don't care what kind of gun you used. Take us back to my truck."

"What? We got some beer to drink, Tony. Don't freak out on me."

"You're crazy."

"Come on, Tony, don't go chicken on me."

"It's not being chicken. It's being stupid. I don't want the beer and I'm telling you right now we're getting out of here."

"All right, all right."

"You okay back there, Woody?" Tony asked.

"Sure," Woody barely managed to say. He wanted to inform his older brother that he thought he was an idiot for getting in Garth's car to begin with, but he bit his tongue and avoided more trouble.

They were back in the city, near the college, and the highway had widened into a boulevard. They stopped at a red light and a police car eased alongside them, to Garth's left. His window was down.

From the back seat, Woody heard the words he would never forget. A cop said loudly, "Stop right there, kid."

Suddenly, there were blue lights everywhere.

CHAPTER 3

A thick cop kept growling, "Shut up, kid. Shut up, kid." But Garth kept talking over his shoulder. He was on the hood of his car, facedown, hands cuffed behind him, feet off the ground. Tony was standing behind the Mustang, also handcuffed, quietly answering questions from two policemen. There seemed to be a dozen of them milling about, poking through Garth's car, huddling with one another, listening to their phones. Radios squawked and a hundred blue lights lit up the intersection. Traffic was blocked in several lanes and a uniformed officer pointed this way and that. A crowd was gathering on a sidewalk, everyone curious to know what terrible crime had been committed by the three young hoodlums.

In the back seat of a patrol car, Woody sat alone and felt very small. His hands were cuffed behind his back. They were snug on his wrists and quite uncomfortable. But, at the moment, he figured that a little pain from the handcuffs was not his biggest problem.

The cops had yanked him out of the car and at first shoved him around, the usual routine, but when they realized he was just a kid, they relaxed and searched him. They took his cell phone, slapped the cuffs on him, and put him in the back seat where he had a decent view of the action. Garth wanted to resist and explain and make it all go away, but the more he talked the rougher the cops became. Tony seemed too frightened to argue with the police.

The crowd continued to gather and Woody tried to slide lower. He watched as Tony was led to another patrol car and placed in the rear seat. Then Garth was removed from the hood of his car and sort of dragged to yet another patrol car and shoved in, talking away the whole time. With the three suspects secured, the police waved over a tow truck with its yellow and orange lights blinking wildly.

To Woody, it seemed like a little too much muscle and manpower just for three stupid kids drinking beer. Still, he knew he was in trouble.

Two policemen got in the front seat and slammed the doors. "You okay, kid?" one asked.

"Yes, sir," Woody answered quickly. Everything had been "yes, sir" and "no, sir" since the moment he'd seen the blue lights.

"We gotta take you to the police station, son," the driver said as he drove away from the scene. The Mustang's front tires were off the ground and the tow truck driver was pulling levers.

"Yes, sir," Woody said. "I guess we should call my mom."

"We'll call her from the station. We got her number from your brother."

"I don't suppose you guys could just take me home could you?"

Both laughed. Short little humorous grunts that quickly passed.

"A comedian," the driver said.

Woody said, "I mean, you know, it's just a little beer."

"A little beer?" the cop in the passenger seat repeated. He turned around, glared at Woody, and growled, "Son, we're talking armed robbery."

A sharp pain hit Woody deep in the gut. He tried to say something—he wasn't sure what—but his throat suddenly clamped shut and his mouth was dry. He managed to breathe and felt sweat under his arms.

Was this a joke, he wanted to ask, but it was obvious

that it was not. Were they really charging him with armed robbery? Surely not. He and Tony had never left the car at the convenience store. How can you pull an armed robbery with a water pistol? It was only a water pistol, right? Woody's shirt was still wet! He had the proof!

He breathed deep and said, "It was only a water pistol."

"That's not what he told the guy at the store," the driver said.

"My shirt is still wet," Woody said, and he realized how stupid he sounded.

"Just shut up, kid," the other cop said.

And he did. And he bit his lip to keep from crying.

At the police station, Woody was led through a side door and into a large reception area where other cops and clerks stopped and gawked at him as if he'd committed a murder. There was no sign of either Tony or Garth. Woody was taken to a room where his handcuffs were removed. A gruff, angry sergeant in a tight uniform growled, "Stand over there, kid. This is your mug shot." Woody backed against a wall, stared at a camera, and for a split second thought of all the bad mug shots of famous people he'd seen online. "Don't smile, kid," the cop said.

"I'm not smiling," Woody said. He had not smiled in days.

"On three. One, two, three." The camera clicked. The

sergeant looked at a screen and said, “Beautiful. Make your mom proud. Sit over there.”

Woody went to a chair and did as he was told. The sergeant took a step over, looked down with a frown, and said, “So they say you’ve been drinking beer, right?”

“Yes, sir.”

“How much?”

“Two cans.”

“Gee, I’ve never heard that before. Every drunk who comes in here says he had just two drinks. How old are you?”

“Thirteen.”

“I need to check your blood alcohol level. We use a machine called a Breathalyzer. Ever heard of it?”

“No, sir.”

“First I need you to agree to it, understand?”

“Not really.”

“You need to sign this consent form which allows us to use a Breathalyzer to measure how much alcohol is in your system. Follow me?”

“Yes, sir.”

“Sign right here.” The sergeant handed down a clipboard with a pen. Woody signed his name by a large X. His hand was shaking so wildly he couldn’t read his own name.

"Should I ask my mom about this?" he asked as he handed the clipboard back.

"Your mum's not here, is she?"

"No, and I'd like to call her but those other policemen took my phone."

"Standard procedure," the sergeant said as he rolled over a cart with the Breathalyzer. He flipped a switch, glanced at a small monitor, then shoved a small tube in Woody's face. "Now, stick this in your mouth and blow as hard as you can."

Woody did as instructed. He blew a second time, then a third, and when the sergeant was finally satisfied he grabbed the tube and hit another switch.

"How'd I do?" Woody asked, breathing heavily as his heart pounded away.

"Great, kid. Point zero six. Not legally drunk but enough to nail you for underage drinking. Now stand up and turn around."

Woody got to his feet and the sergeant slapped the handcuffs onto his wrists. He was led from the room and down a hallway where the two detectives were waiting. The sergeant said, "He's all yours. Point zero six."

The detectives took him down some stairs to a small windowless room where he was told to sit in a chair and say nothing. They just left him there. He had not seen Tony or Garth since they had driven away from the street. He waited and waited and had no idea of the time. He wanted to call his mother because she would be worried, and he really needed her at that awful moment.

There was no one to help him. A thirteen-year-old kid locked away in the basement of the police station and no one to help.

Tony was in a similar room two doors down, though neither knew where his brother was at the moment. Garth was also in the basement, just down the hall.

Two detectives in plainclothes walked into Garth's room, closed the door, and pulled chairs up to the narrow table. The first one said, "You're eighteen years old so we're treating you like an adult. You ever been arrested before?"

Garth knew it was all a misunderstanding and his father would have it cleared up by sunrise. So, he had nothing to worry about. "Couple of times," he said without concern. "But nothing serious. Youth Court stuff."

"This ain't Youth Court, son. This is the real thing. We need to ask you some questions."

"Okay, but don't you have to read me my rights, like they always do on television?"

"Sure. You have the right to remain silent. Anything you

say can be used against you in court. And you have the right to an attorney. Understand?"

"Don't I get a phone call? I really want to call my dad."

"Later. Where did you get the pistol?"

"What pistol?"

The second detective pulled out a clear plastic bag and laid it on the table. He said, "Looks just like a nine millimeter Ruger. Could've fooled me. Certainly fooled the guy at the convenience store."

"Where'd you get it?" the first detective asked again.

"The kid gave it to me. It's his. What—you think I go around shooting water pistols? It's the kid's."

"Woody's?"

"Sure. Not mine."

Garth believed that if he and Tony stuck together and blamed it all on Woody, a thirteen-year-old kid, then they could walk away free as birds and nothing much would happen to Woody. Anyway, it was just a little fun and games and his father would handle it soon enough.

"Who planned the robbery?" the second detective asked.

"I really want to talk to my dad. He'll get a lawyer. If that's okay?"

"Whose idea was it to rob the convenience store?"

"No one's. You see, it really wasn't a robbery because it

was just a water pistol. It was sort of a joke, you know? This is all one big misunderstanding and my dad and his lawyer will clear up everything. You guys need to relax a little."

"So it was your idea?"

"Look, you said I could remain silent, right? And that I can have a lawyer. Okay, I want to call my dad and he'll bring in a lawyer."

"How much money did you take?"

"I'm not talking anymore."

The detectives finally left the room. They chatted briefly in the hallway, then entered the room where young Woody was waiting, terrified by now.

They sat down, both scowling as if they were about to interrogate a serial killer, and the first one said, "We've talked to your brother Tony and your pal Garth. Both of them swear that the pistol belongs to you."

Woody felt like he'd been hit in the head with a brick. "What?" he managed to say, in shock. His jaw dropped and his eyes watered, and he looked at the first detective in total disbelief. Why would Tony say something like that? Why would both of them lie to the police and try to pin the blame on him?

"You heard me, kid," the first detective said. "Your buddies are saying it's your gun."

"It's just a water pistol."

"The guy at the store didn't think so. Under our law it's armed robbery. Twenty plus years for your two buddies, off to the juvenile joint for you. But if you tell us the truth, we'll lean on the judge to cut you some slack. Know what I mean?"

"Not really."

"We know the judge, he knows us. If you tell us everything, we can put in a good word with him and you'll get off light."

"What do you want to know?" Woody asked slowly. Something told him not to say too much to the police, but then he was terrified at the moment and wanted to help.

"Whose gun is it?"

"Garth's. Tony and I never saw it until he came back to the car. We didn't go into the store. Look at the security cameras. We had no idea what Garth was doing. He just wanted some more beer, and so he drove to the store, told us to wait for a minute, went inside, came back with a case of beer, and after we were driving away he pulled out the pistol and laughed about robbing the guy. That's what happened. I swear. Tony and I knew nothing."

"How long had you guys been drinking beer?"

"I don't know. Tony and I delivered pizza, then bumped

into Garth. I knew it was a mistake to go cruising with him. He had some beer and really wanted me to drink some. I can't stand the stuff, but I was trying to, you know, be cool, like the big guys."

Woody's voice cracked and his lip quivered.

The detectives exchanged looks. The first one said, "Cool like the big guys. We see it all the time. That'll get you some jail time."

CHAPTER 4

Daisy Lambert turned into her driveway at 11:15, and she immediately noticed that Tony's little blue truck was not parked where it was supposed to be. It wasn't there. The house was completely dark, not a single light in any window. The boys always waited for her to get home from work before they went to bed.

For a moment, she sat in her car and prayed that nothing was wrong, then got out. Inside the house, she found nothing—not a note, not a sign of either son. She had called and texted both of them driving home. Neither responded, but that was not that unusual. Often, late at night, the boys ignored their phones.

She turned on lights, called them again, and fixed a pot of coffee. It was probably going to be a long night.

She called her husband, who was two hours away with his work crew, woke him up, and told him the boys were not home. They were not his boys, but rather his stepsons, and there was nothing he could do at that moment. He suggested she call the police.

The minutes passed slowly, and Daisy sat in the den with a cup of coffee and watched the front yard. She prayed that any minute the little blue truck would arrive and her boys would be safe. She wanted to see headlights. It was midnight now and there was no traffic on their narrow street at the edge of Strattenburg. The next lights would be her boys, she just knew it.

At midnight, she called the police station but no one there had ever heard of the Lambert boys. She tried to sit in the den again but was too anxious. She poured another cup and went for a drive around town, looking for Tony's truck, looking for red and blue lights at the scene of some terrible car wreck, looking for any sign of them, and waiting for her phone to ring. She stopped by Santo's but it was closed.

After roaming through the empty streets for an hour, she saw two police cars in the parking lot of a motel. Their lights were on, their engines running, the policemen sharing some late night gossip. She parked nearby and nervously approached the two cars. She asked for their help. She explained her situation, and, in tears, asked if they could do anything. The policemen said sure and called the dispatcher on his radio. Within minutes word came back that the Lambert boys were in custody.

And charged with armed robbery.

When Daisy arrived at the city jail she found her way to the night desk where the dispatcher was drinking coffee while waiting on 911 calls and radio reports from the patrol cars. A night clerk sat at a nearby table and asked what she wanted. She identified herself and said that her two sons were in jail, and she was there to take them home. The night clerk frowned and asked her to have a seat across the room in a row of old plastic chairs. There was no one else around at that hour. She sat down and began chewing her nails, a nervous habit that kept her from crying, though she had cried all the way to the station.

Armed robbery? There must be some mistake. Random thoughts raced through her mind and she couldn't control them. None were good. Smoking pot, drinking beer, driving while drunk, fighting, maybe shoplifting or petty theft—these were the small crimes that she might have expected. Sure, they were bad enough, but a lot of kids got in trouble for them and most survived.

But armed robbery? To her knowledge, Tony did not own a gun. He was only seventeen! Her husband—the boys' stepfather—was not a hunter and did not keep rifles in the house. He owned two pistols that she knew of. One he kept hidden in their closet for self-defense and the other he kept in the glove box in his truck. The boys had never touched either weapon. How would Tony get a gun? Then, why would he use it to rob someone? And why would he involve his little brother?

The thought of Woody sitting in a jail cell broke her heart again and she began to cry, as softly as possible.

A jolly old deputy sat down beside her. He had a mass of gray hair that scattered in all directions, and plump rosy cheeks, and if he switched uniforms he could have easily passed for Santa Claus. "Now, now, it's not that bad," he said. "The boys are safe."

Daisy wiped her nose and asked, "How do you know?"

"I'm the jailer and I'm in charge of all inmates, including the juveniles. Randolph's my name. And you're Mrs. Lambert?"

Randolph glanced at his clipboard.

"I am. Where are they now?"

"We keep the kids in a separate wing. They're in a cell together, with no one else."

"When can I get them out?"

"Well, not tonight. They'll go before a judge in the morning, and he'll set their bail. Do you understand bail?"

"Yes, I've been through this before, not long ago. Tony was arrested and I had to put up some money for his bail. Fortunately, it wasn't very much and we got him out. But I'm broke now. How much is his bail?"

"Armed robbery is pretty serious, so I'd expect it to be high."

"What kind of armed robbery? Can you tell me what they did? This is insane."

"I don't know the facts, ma'am. Just what's in the report here. There were three of them, your boys and a kid named Garth Tucker. Looks like he was the driver. All I know is that they supposedly robbed a convenience store on the western edge of town."

"A convenience store?"

"Yes, you know, one of those little grocery stores with gas pumps out front, stays open late at night."

"I know what a convenience store is. Why would they rob a convenience store?"

"Oh, I don't know. Maybe it was convenient." Randolph chuckled at his cleverness. Daisy glared at him as if he were an idiot. "Sorry," he said. "Look, Mrs. Lambert, you can't do anything right now, so it's best to go home and get some rest."

"Rest? I won't sleep a wink. Can I at least see them? Woody is only thirteen."

"Sorry, ma'am, but we have rules regarding visitation. Trust me, though, both boys are safe. And by the way, they're good boys. I've talked to them."

"I guess I should say thanks but that doesn't quite feel right. After all, they're charged with armed robbery."

"And underage drinking."

"Of course. Anything else?"

"Not that I know of."

"Why didn't they call me? They both had phones."

"Well, I'm not sure about that. The phones were confiscated when they were arrested, standard procedure." Randolph flipped through his paperwork. "Don't know why they were not allowed to call home. Somebody else must've screwed up."

"Screwed up? These are my kids we're talking about. Where are their phones now?"

"In custody. They can't have phones in their cells. Another rule."

"A lot of rules around here and none of them seem to be working. It's pretty rotten that you don't allow a thirteen-year-old boy to call his mother when he's being thrown in jail."

"You're right. I agree. I'll speak to my supervisor. Sorry about that."

"You're sorry that somebody else screwed up. This is insane. Why can't I talk to them now?"

"Because it's almost two in the morning. Lights out at midnight back there. I'm sorry, ma'am, but at least your boys are safe."

"Safe? Forgive me but things don't seem too safe right now."

"I understand, ma'am. Why don't you leave and come back in a few hours? You can see them then."

"I'll just sit here, okay? If I go home I'll just walk the floors. Is it okay to stay here and read magazines until sunrise."

"Sure. Would you like some coffee?"

She managed to smile and said, "Yes, that would be nice. Thank you."

The cell had three walls of concrete and one of metal bars. Bunk beds were attached to the rear wall. Tony arrived first and claimed the bottom bunk. Woody climbed onto the top one. All lights went out at midnight when everyone was supposed to go to sleep. However, in the darkness, it seemed like everyone wanted to talk. There was laughter in the distance, some yelling. As Woody was walked down the hall, he glanced into the other cells. All appeared to be juveniles, though a couple looked as mean as any veteran criminal. In one cell, a boy of no more than ten sat by himself.

Tony denied pinning the ownership of the pistol on Woody. Indeed, Tony had not even been interviewed by the police. Nor had he seen any sign of Garth. Whispering in the darkness, the brothers agreed to stick together, and stick to the truth. Why would they not tell the truth? Garth was a moron who'd pulled a stupid stunt. He honestly thought he could stick a gun in someone's face, demand cash and beer, make his getaway, and laugh everything off as a joke.

As the minutes became hours, the laughter and yelling died down. Slowly, the conversations did, too. At some point during the awful night, Woody realized Tony was asleep.

CHAPTER 5

Mr. Mount called his homeroom to order when the bell rang at 8:45. Of his sixteen students, fifteen were present. Woody was not, which Theo had noticed immediately. It wasn't that unusual. No one was missing more school these days than Woody.

The class went through the usual morning routine of discussing the day's activities. Science projects were due. The Debate Team had a match in one week. Band practice, soccer practice, rehearsals for the eighth-grade play. As always, the mood was light as Mr. Mount believed in starting each day on an encouraging note. He would see them again during third period for his Government class.

When the bell rang for first period, the boys grabbed

their backpacks and hustled into the hallway. Mr. Mount asked Theo to hang back for a moment. When they were alone, he said, gravely, "Look, Theo, Woody's mother stopped by the school earlier and informed Mrs. Gladwell that Woody got arrested last night."

Theo's mouth fell open. "Arrested?"

"Yes. He's in jail and due in court this morning. Mrs. Gladwell wants you to hurry down to Youth Court and see what's going on. You're excused for the morning." He handed Theo a slip of paper.

Theo took off. He was at once thrilled to be free from classes but also terrified by the news. He left his backpack at the office, raced out the front door, hopped on his bike, and ten minutes later wheeled to a stop in front of the courthouse. As he was entering the main door, Officer Stu Peckinpaw, a truant cop and the terror of all skipping students, stopped him and said, "Well, hello, Theo. Why aren't you in school?"

Theo handed him the slip of paper and said, "Official business."

Officer Peckinpaw examined the pass as if reading an important document. He handed it back and said, "Okay, but I'd better not see you on the streets after lunch."

"Yes, sir." Theo ducked inside and bounded up the stairs. He knew every inch of the courthouse and knew exactly where to find Woody. Juvenile matters were handled in a small, cramped courtroom on the second floor where Judge Frank Pendergrast had presided for many years. At the door, Theo took a deep breath and stepped inside.

Because Youth Court was private and all hearings were conducted without juries, the courtroom was small, with only two rows for spectators. Even Animal Court down in the basement had more room.

Theo saw Daisy Lambert sitting in the front row and went straight to her. Judge Pendergrast was not on the bench. Bailiff Trench, the ancient courtroom deputy, nodded at Theo.

"What's going on?" Theo whispered to Mrs. Lambert.

She smiled but her eyes were red and she looked exhausted. She was obviously glad to see Theo. "I don't know, Theo," she said in a soft voice. "Woody and Tony got arrested last night for armed robbery. They wouldn't let me see them. It's just so awful."

"Armed robbery?" Theo repeated. "You gotta be kidding. But what happened?"

"I don't know. They wouldn't tell me much."

They whispered for a long time as other worried parents drifted in. Bailiff Trench eased over to inform them that Judge Pendergrast was running a bit late, which was not unusual.

At ten o'clock, a door opened behind the bench and Judge Pendergrast appeared in his black robe. He assumed his position, glanced around the room, and said, "I apologize for being late. I got almost no sleep last night because every dog on the street was barking and howling." He noticed Theo sitting in the front row and said, "Well, hello, Theo. Good to see you as always. What brings you here?"

Without standing—things were quite relaxed in Youth Court—Theo said, "My friend Woody Lambert is on the docket."

"Oh, I see. Well, let's bring him in." Bailiff Trench opened a side door. Woody and Tony were escorted in by a policeman who removed their handcuffs. Both boys looked at their mother and shook their heads. Daisy fought back tears. Bailiff Trench herded the boys to a spot directly in front of the bench. They looked up at His Honor, who looked down at them with a frown and said, "Okay, this is a first appearance for Mr. Tony Lambert, age seventeen, and Mr. Woodrow Lambert, age thirteen, both charged with armed robbery, along with Mr. Garth Tucker, who is eighteen and thus will be dealt with over in Circuit Court."

He looked at Daisy and asked, "Can I assume you're their mother?"

"Yes, sir," Daisy said, wiping her eyes.

"These are very serious charges and I don't see an

attorney present, other than, of course, Mr. Theodore Boone, who is a pretty good lawyer but a bit too young to be admitted to the bar. Do you plan to hire a lawyer, Mrs., uh, Mrs.—"

"Lambert, Daisy Lambert," she said. "I can't afford a lawyer."

"Okay. Without a lawyer, I'm not going to ask these boys any questions right now. The public defender's office will provide lawyers for them and that will be done today, if possible. Given the seriousness of these charges, I'm not going to proceed until they have lawyers."

Without thinking and without hesitating, Theo stood and said, "Your Honor, if I may, do you mind if I say something?"

Judge Pendergrast glared down over the top of the reading glasses perched halfway down his nose. "Why aren't you in school, Theo?" he asked.

"I have a pass signed by Mrs. Gladwell, Judge. Can I say that I know this family very well? Woody is one of my best friends. We're in the same grade, same class, same Boy Scout troop. We've been close friends for years. Just like you, I don't know what happened last night but I can promise you that Woody and Tony Lambert had nothing to do with an armed robbery. Right now they are innocent until proven guilty. That's the way our system works, right, Your Honor?"

"Where are you going with this, Theo?"

"They have the right to bail, to get out of jail while everything is sorted out. Frankly, at least in my opinion, they don't need to post bail because bail just makes sure they will show up in court when they are supposed to. I can promise you that Tony and Woody will always show up in court."

"You want me to just release them?"

"Yes, sir. Why not? They're not criminals. They're not guilty, I can assure you of that."

"Do you know the facts, Theo?"

"Not really, but I know these two guys, especially Woody."

"I'm sorry, Theo, but it's too early for that. Let's wait until they have lawyers and then we can discuss the issue of bail. You may sit down."

Theo sat down slowly and mumbled, "Thanks."

Judge Pendergrast continued. "Let's get all the paperwork straight and let me talk to the prosecutor and police. In the meantime, the public defender's office will get involved and we'll meet back here as soon as possible. Bailiff, please take these two back to the jail until further orders."

Theo and Daisy watched the officer slap the cuffs back onto the wrists of Woody and Tony. As they left, Woody turned and said over his shoulder, "Thanks, Theo." When they were gone, Daisy began sobbing quietly.

"Nice job, Theo," Judge Pendergrast said. "But from now on let's wait until you pass the bar exam and get a license to practice law, okay?"

"Yes, sir. And thanks, Judge."

"You're excused and I suggest you find your way back to school real soon."

"Yes, sir."

Theo and Daisy quickly left the courtroom and found a seat on a bench in the hallway. Theo glanced around to make sure no one was listening and asked, "Do you know where the jail is?"

"Are you kidding? I just spent the night there. I wish I'd never seen the place."

"Okay. Let's get over there and try to meet with them."

"Thanks, Theo."

Along with the judges and lawyers, Theo knew most of the policemen in Strattenburg. He arrived at the station first and went straight to the desk of a captain named Rick Pruitt. Theo's mother had handled an adoption for Captain Pruitt and Theo knew him well.

The captain was plowing through a stack of paperwork and was surprised to see his young friend. "Well, hello, Theo. Shouldn't you be in school?"

"I'm excused until noon. Important business. My friend got arrested last night and he's back there in the jail. His mother has not been allowed to see him or his brother, and I need your help."

"What's his name?" Pruitt asked as he picked up the daily arrest sheet.

"Lambert. Woody and Tony Lambert."

"Armed robbery?"

"Yes, sir, but it's a big misunderstanding, at least I think so. We just need to see him, me and his mother."

"And underage drinking?"

"Not so sure about that, but Judge Pendergrast wouldn't set a bail this morning, so they're still locked up. We just want to visit them and see what's going on."

Pruitt frowned at Theo for a few seconds, then stood and said, "Follow me."

They went down a hallway, then down the stairs to the jail. The waiting room was filling up with relatives checking on other inmates. Pruitt pointed to some chairs and said, "Have a seat."

Theo sat down and within minutes Daisy arrived. In a whisper, Theo explained what was going on. A few minutes later, Pruitt returned and said, "Wait here. It'll take a few minutes."

"Thanks, Captain," Theo said, and Pruitt disappeared.

They waited half an hour before a jailer called Daisy's name. She and Theo followed him to a holding room where he unlocked the door and waved them in. Woody and Tony were seated at a table, without handcuffs, and when they saw their mother both jumped to their feet. The jailer closed the door and waited outside.

After a round of hugs and tears, all four pulled chairs around a table.

Woody and Tony told their story.

CHAPTER 6

When Theo had heard enough, he decided to leave the family alone and run a quick mission. On his bike, he raced back to the courthouse and went to the Office of the Public Defender on the third floor.

The head PD was a lawyer named Don Montgomery, but everybody called him Monk. To the other lawyers, judges, policemen, and courthouse clerks he was simply Monk. Theo had seen him in the courtroom on several occasions and no one used his real name. It was "Yes, Monk" and "No, Monk" and "Your turn, Monk." Of course when juries were present and things were more formal, he became Mr. Montgomery, but that was rare. On one occasion the Boone family had bumped into him and his wife in a restaurant, and both of Theo's parents addressed him as Monk.

He had a difficult job, one that few lawyers envied. His office represented men and women charged with serious crimes but not enough money to hire lawyers. And since the Supreme Court had ruled that every defendant is entitled to a lawyer, Stratten County had created, long before Theo was born, the Office of the Public Defender.

Monk's operation was always swamped with too many clients and not enough staff to serve them. Every year Monk asked the county for more money, and it seemed, at least to Theo, that he was never satisfied with the support he received. According to Woods Boone, Theo's father, most PD offices in the country were run on thin budgets. Politicians gave them a low priority because they didn't like to spend money on criminal defendants.

Theo hesitated before going inside. He paused and sent a text to Mr. Mount. Found Woody. He's still in jail. Charges seem silly but still serious. Be back soon.

A secretary sat behind an old desk that was covered with stacks of files. Metal cabinets lined the walls. She was typing and paused long enough to frown at him, and without a smile she said, "Yes?"

"Hello, I'm Theodore Boone and I'm looking for Mr. Montgomery."

"Why aren't you in school?"

"I'm excused for a few hours. You see, my friend got arrested last night and his case will be assigned to this office. It's a Youth Court matter and I would like to see Mr. Montgomery."

"He's in a big trial in the main courtroom, Judge Gantry. Youth Court matters are handled by Rodney Wall."

Theo did not know that lawyer. "Okay, could I please see Mr. Wall?"

"He hasn't come in yet."

"When might he come in?"

"I don't know. I'm not in charge of his schedule. Look, son, I'm very busy. You can check back later." She returned to her keyboard and resumed typing. Theo backed away and left the office. He walked down to the second floor and went to the office of Judge Henry Gantry, the senior Circuit Court judge and a pal of Theo's.

When he was dreaming, which seemed like several hours each day, Theo wanted to be a respected courtroom judge like Henry Gantry, a man of great fairness and wisdom.

Judge Gantry's secretary was Mrs. Hardy, a sweet lady who was always happy to see him, unlike that woman upstairs in Monk's office.

"Well, hello, Theo," Mrs. Hardy said as he interrupted her work. "To what do we owe this honor?"

"I need to see the judge."

"Of course. And shouldn't you be in school?"

"Everyone seems to think so. I'm excused by the principal. You see, one of my friends got arrested last night and I'm trying to help him."

"How old is he?"

"Only thirteen. I know, it's a Youth Court matter, but I still need to see the judge."

"Well, he's tied up right now. We're in the middle of a big trial and he's meeting with the lawyers."

"What kind of trial?"

Mrs. Hardy glanced around as if someone else might be listening, as if the trial were a big secret. "It's a drug case. Some men from out in the county were caught manufacturing drugs."

"Is Mr. Monk defending the guys?"

"How'd you know?"

"I just left his office. I don't suppose I could watch the trial, could I? I'm excused from school until noon."

"That's up to you, Theo. The courtroom is open to the public, but if Judge Gantry sees you he might not like it."

"Good point. Thanks, Mrs. Hardy." Theo walked to the door but stopped when he thought of something else. "Say,

Mrs. Hardy, when does Judge Gantry set bail for new defendants, for guys who've just been arrested?"

"Usually, it's the first thing he does in the morning. Doesn't take long."

"A guy got arrested last night for armed robbery, name's Garth Tucker, eighteen years old. Have you seen his paperwork?"

Without looking for a file, she said, "Sure. Judge Gantry set his bail at fifty thousand dollars."

"Fifty thousand dollars?"

"Yes. It's a serious crime."

"Of course it is, but bail wouldn't be that high for a juvenile, would it?"

"Oh, I don't know, Theo. Bail is usually lower for juveniles, but that's another court."

"Yes, ma'am. Thanks. See you later."

"Get to school."

Mr. Tucker had arrived at the jail at eight a.m., after a sleepless night, and his lawyer was not far behind. When the jailer received the confirmation that bail had been set, a bail bondsman was quickly called and hustled over from his shabby office across the street. The arrangement was typical. For a 10 percent fee, the bondsman produced a written guarantee that Garth would remain in the county and show up for court when required. Mr. Tucker wrote a check for $5,000 and left the jail with his son. They went to the city pound, paid another fee of $250, and Garth drove his Mustang home. An hour later, after a shower and change of clothes, he was at school bragging about his big adventure.

By then, Woody and Tony were back in their cell playing checkers, the only game available, and killing time. Daisy was at work, cutting hair in a salon. Theo was watching the clock and trying to keep out of sight. If one more adult mentioned school he might explode.

At 11:30, he swallowed hard and reentered the PD's office, certain that the grouchy secretary would yell at him. She did not. She quietly informed him that attorney Rodney Wall had called and was investigating a case over in Masseyville, a small town half an hour away. He wasn't sure when he would make it to the courthouse, if at all.

The office had only three lawyers. Monk, Rodney Wall, and a guy named Udall, who was assisting Monk in the drug trial. So there were no lawyers left behind in the office, and no one for Theo to plead with. Defeated, he said thanks to the secretary and rode back to school.

During lunch, he met with Mr. Mount and Mrs. Gladwell and explained the situation. The charges against Woody and Tony would probably be reduced or dismissed, at least the armed robbery, but they would stay in jail until their lawyer could convince Judge Pendergrast to set a reasonable bail.

"It's pretty outrageous," Theo said.

"But it's not that unusual," Mr. Mount said. "Our juvenile system is overloaded and there are never enough lawyers and counselors. It's not unusual for kids to get chewed up by the system. Woody will be lucky if he doesn't spend time in a detention center, which are not good places."

"But he didn't do anything," Theo said.

"He's an accomplice to a crime," Mr. Mount said. He had once been a lawyer and gave up that profession to teach.

"Can you explain that?" Mrs. Gladwell asked.

"It's the law everywhere," Mr. Mount said. "Pretty basic stuff, really. Three guys are together. One has a gun. He goes in, pulls the gun, grabs the loot or whatever, and all three make their getaway. The two who waited in the car will always be charged with being accomplices to the robbery and will face the same punishment."

"That's not right," Theo said.

"Well, not in this case. But Woody is in serious trouble. I doubt if he'll get off free on this one. It's pretty heavy stuff, Theo."

"With a water pistol?"

"I'm assuming the guy who got robbed didn't know it

was just a water pistol. I'll bet his story is that he thought it was a real gun. That's all that matters. What a stupid move."

"Do you know this guy, Garth Tucker?" Mrs. Gladwell asked Theo.

"I don't know him but I've heard of him. He's one of Tony's friends, though Tony claims they didn't hang out that much. Woody told me and his mother that he has never liked Garth, said he always thought the guy was trouble. Woody thinks Garth was probably drunker than they realized."

"He must not be very smart," Mr. Mount said.

"And Woody was drinking, too?" Mrs. Gladwell asked.

"He had a couple of beers."

"Does he do this a lot?"

Theo didn't know how much beer Woody was drinking, and that didn't matter at the moment. He wasn't about to squeal on his buddy. "I don't think so," he said. "I've never seen him do it. But he and Tony are alone a good bit. Their stepfather works out of town and their mother has two or three jobs. Things are not going too well around their house."

"That poor kid," she said. "Sitting in jail with no one to help him."

CHAPTER 7

Theo suffered through the afternoon, watching the clocks in his classrooms and thinking of nothing but Woody in jail. When the final bell rang, he sprinted to the small auditorium where the Debate Team was gathering for a practice session. Mr. Mount coached them. Theo was the captain, but he was in no mood to practice. He whispered to Mr. Mount that he had an idea to help Woody and needed to skip the session.

"I'm going straight to my mom and insist that she go to court to see the judge," he said.

"But she doesn't work in Youth Court," Mr. Mount said quietly.

"I know, but I can beg her for a favor. And it's getting

late in the day. If we don't do something fast, Woody will spend another night in jail."

"Take off," Mr. Mount said, and Theo disappeared. Ten minutes later he slid to a stop in the gravel lot behind Boone & Boone. He burst through the rear door and into the small room he called his office. Judge was nowhere in sight. Vince, the paralegal, and Dorothy, the real estate secretary, were not in their offices. The door to his mother's office was closed, which of course meant she was meeting with a client. Theo walked to Elsa's desk and braced himself for the daily ritual of hugs and questions. But she was on the phone and couldn't grab him. She smiled, indicated that the call might take some time, and sort of waved him off. Judge aroused from his slumbers and stumbled forth for a good head-scratching. But Theo was too busy. He bounded up the stairs to confront his father, but Woods Boone was gone, too.

At times the place was packed, with meetings everywhere and clients waiting in chairs. At other times, it was deserted. Theo, with Judge close behind, went downstairs where Elsa was hanging up. "I need to see my mother right now," he demanded.

Elsa could tell he was in no mood for small talk. "She's with a client. What's going on?"

Theo gave her the quick version of Woody's troubles

and ended with, "I want my mom to go to Youth Court right now and help Woody."

"Well, your mother is with a client who's having a bad day."

All of her clients had bad days. Almost all were women struggling through divorces. Most of them arrived stressed and left in tears. Theo had learned to avoid the front section of the firm when his mother was with a client. He had actually heard them in her office crying.

"I'm not going to interrupt them," Elsa said, somewhat sternly. She was the sweetest person Theo knew, but he also knew that when she dug in, she was not going to budge.

"Then I'm going in there."

"No you're not. I suggest you wait until four o'clock when the meeting is over."

Theo retreated to his office, with his dog, and unpacked his backpack. Homework was out of the question. He opened his laptop, found Garth's Facebook page, and quickly learned that the kid was out of jail and laughing about his arrest.

Theo fumed some more as the minutes dragged by. Four o'clock came and went without a word. He eased to the front and hid in the large conference room, waiting for his mother's door to open. When it finally did, a well-dressed woman stepped out, wiping her eyes, and left without a word. Theo rushed in and said, "Mom, Woody got arrested last night and he's still in jail. You gotta go help him."

Mrs. Boone calmly closed the door and pointed to a leather sofa. Theo sat down and took a deep breath. Of all the many things he admired about his mother, her coolness under pressure was the most impressive. Marcella Boone was never rattled. She spent long hours every day dealing with extremely anxious clients, and demanding judges, and tough lawyers on the other side, and she rarely lost her cool. And, when her only child was troubled, she found the time to listen.

Theo told her everything he knew about Woody's big adventure. She, too, was stunned and worried about him and Tony. "You've been concerned about Woody," she said.

"Sure, and things are worse now. Why can't you go over to Youth Court and ask Judge Pendergrast to set bail. You know him, don't you?"

"Of course I do, Theo, but I don't represent Woody. As you know, I don't handle criminal matters."

"He's not a criminal, Mom."

"No, he is not, but he's in the middle of a criminal mess, and for the time being he will be processed through Youth Court."

"Look, Mom, it's not unusual for one lawyer to handle one hearing and then another take over the case for the later stuff, right?"

"I suppose," she said, but she knew he was right.

"Then let's go see Judge Pendergrast, ask him to set bail, as low as possible, and get Woody out. Then tomorrow or the next day the public defender will take over and defend Woody."

Mrs. Boone glanced away, and Theo knew he was onto something. She stood, walked to her desk, picked up the phone, punched some numbers. Looking at Theo, she said, "Yes, this is Marcella Boone, attorney, and I'm looking for Judge Pendergrast. I need to speak to him."

She listened, glanced at her watch, and asked, "What time will he be in tomorrow?"

She listened, nodded, said, "Please ask him to call me in the morning."

She hung up and said, "He's gone for the day."

Theo said, "It's barely four thirty. How can the guy leave so early? That means Woody and Tony have to spend another night in jail. This is ridiculous."

"Judges have heavy dockets, and then some days are lighter. If there's nothing to do, they often leave a bit early. Judge Pendergrast is a hard worker."

Theo dropped his head and shoulders and gave up. Elsa

tapped on the door as she opened it and said, "Your four thirty appointment is here."

"Thank you," Mrs. Boone said. "We'll discuss this later, Theo. Now go do your homework."

Dinner was a soggy sandwich on stale white bread, a banana, a thin marshmallow pie, and a carton of warm apple juice. Woody and Tony devoured it while complaining to each other about it, but they were hungry. Lunch had been a cold pasta concoction they'd had trouble choking down. Breakfast was hours away.

A television hung from the ceiling at the end of the hallway, but they could not see it. Not that they really wanted to. Game shows were at full volume and the noise was oddly comforting. The noise reminded them that life somewhere was normal.

The hours passed slowly. The television was turned off. A guard walked through and announced that lights would go out in thirty minutes. Two more guards appeared with a new prisoner, an older boy who looked well beyond eighteen years. They stopped at the door, unlocked it, and shoved him inside with Tony and Woody. The cell had two bunk beds, no more.

When the guards left, the new guy said, "I'm Jock, and you're?"

"I'm Tony. This is my kid brother, Woody." There was no effort to shake hands. Jock had the look of a kid with an attitude, a tough dude who'd seen several jails from the inside. He looked at the bunks and said, "I'll take the top one, if that's okay?"

"That's mine," Woody said. "First come, first served."

"Oh really? And who's making the rules around here?"

"The guards," Tony said.

"Don't see any guards right now. Look, I'll make this real simple for you two brothers. If you want to start some crap, let's get it over with. I'll take on the two of you right now, and I promise you that within thirty seconds you'll both be on the floor, spitting blood and missing teeth. Is that what you want?" He suddenly shoved Tony hard and he banged into a concrete wall.

There was little doubt that Jock had been in many more street fights than the Lambert boys. He was lean and hard, with thick arms, one of which had a tattoo on it. He also reeked of alcohol, and his eyes were red and sort of crazed looking.

Tony showed him both palms and said, "Fighting won't solve any problems around here."

"Smart boy," Jock said. He stepped onto the bottom bunk and vaulted onto the top one where he stretched out and closed his eyes.

Tony and Woody looked at each other and shrugged in defeat. Losing a bunk was better than losing some teeth, and Jock seemed eager to throw punches. They settled down into the bottom bunk, Tony on one end, Woody on the other, and tried to make themselves comfortable.

It would be a long night.

CHAPTER 8

Theo didn't sleep much either. He dozed off from time to time but could not stop thinking about Woody behind bars. At midnight, he suddenly thought of something else that bothered him. He went online, checked the local newspaper, and saw a one paragraph story about the armed robbery. An eighteen-year-old named Garth Tucker had been arrested for robbing Kall's Grocery, a convenience store on the western edge of town. Two minors were also involved, but their names were withheld, as was the custom. Tucker was "free on bond."

So, the stupid kid who'd pulled the gun was resting comfortably at home with his family while Woody and Tony were still locked up. What was fair about that? As he stewed and mumbled to himself, Theo found Garth's Facebook page and saw a staged photo of him holding his wrists together with what appeared to be handcuffs. Beside the photo Garth wrote: "Jail ain't so bad but the food's lousy. It's all a big misunderstanding and will soon be cleared up, according to my lawyer."

Theo turned off his laptop and tried to close his eyes. He eventually drifted off, woke up again, went to the bathroom, spoke to Judge under his bed, and tried to go back to sleep. At sunrise, he showered and dressed quickly and hustled downstairs.

He was at the kitchen table pretending to review his homework when his father appeared. Every morning, Mr. Boone rose early, made the coffee, and left to have breakfast with his friends at a downtown diner. When he saw Theo he said, "Well, good morning."

Theo did not respond. He was angry with his parents and they had argued over last night's dinner. As always, they had busy plans for the morning and neither wanted to get involved with Woody's case. Theo did not understand why they, or at least one of them, could not go to Youth Court and insist that Woody and Tony be released immediately. They had tried to explain that they were not criminal lawyers and did not work in Youth Court, but Theo didn't buy it.

If Theo wasn't speaking, then neither was Mr. Boone. He made the coffee, fetched the newspaper out of the driveway, found his briefcase, which he brought home every night but rarely touched, poured a cup, and left without a word.

Theo fumed and watched the clock. There were clocks in every room of their home, clear proof that they were busy people with organized lives. Normally, Mrs. Boone skipped breakfast and instead sipped coffee in the den while flipping through the newspaper. But she was running late. Theo could hear her moving about upstairs. He waited. Judge began whimpering because he wanted breakfast, so Theo fixed him a bowl of cereal with milk, the same meal Theo had every morning.

At eight, Mrs. Boone appeared dressed for work. She wore a pretty maroon dress, black heels, and jewelry. One look and Theo knew she was ready for court. She always dressed fashionably, but there were times when she looked a bit sharper. She poured a cup of coffee and sat across the table from Theo. She said, "I'll meet you in Youth Court at nine. You call Daisy Lambert and I'll call Mrs. Gladwell and tell her what's going on."

Theo exhaled, smiled, and said, "Thanks, Mom." He hurriedly grabbed the bowls and put them in the sink. He rubbed Judge's head, said good-bye, and sprinted from the kitchen with his backpack.

The small courtroom was filled with people when Judge Pendergrast assumed the bench and said good morning. For the second straight morning, he looked exhausted with dark circles under his eyes and fatigue all over his face. He even yawned as he glanced around the courtroom.

An important hearing was scheduled for nine o'clock and Theo was worried that the Lambert boys would be ignored until later. However, his mother had made a phone call and chatted with the judge.

He peered over his reading glasses and said, "Mrs. Boone, I believe you have a matter before the Court."

Marcella Boone stood and everybody looked at her. Theo had seen her in court on several occasions, though she would not allow him to sit through her divorce trials. The testimony was often too rough for a thirteen-year-old. He admired her greatly and knew she could handle herself in front of any judge.

"Yes, Your Honor, thank you, and I would like to enter an appearance as the attorney of record for the sole purpose of getting bail set for Tony and Woody Lambert."

"So you're their lawyer?"

"Sort of. I know the family and I'm just pinch-hitting until the public defender's office can take over."

"Where is the public defender?"

"Good question. I am told that his office has yet to talk

to the Lambert boys. I assume the PD is very busy, as always."

"Well, I was informed by Mrs. Lambert yesterday that she could not afford a lawyer."

"I'm here pro bono, Judge, as a friend of the family, and just for the purposes of getting bail set. We're trying to get the boys out of jail. The PD will take over from there."

Judge Pendergrast yawned again and shrugged, as if he didn't really approve of her involvement, but no judge in the state would tell Marcella Boone that she didn't belong in a courtroom. He said, "Very well. I'll note your appearance. Are the boys here?"

"No, sir. They're still in jail. Their presence is not necessary. It's just a bail hearing, Your Honor."

Judge Pendergrast shuffled some papers and read something. "Each is charged with armed robbery. What type of bail are you requesting?"

"Personal ID, Your Honor. The Lamberts have lived here for many years, and there is no reason to believe that Woody and Tony will not appear in court when they are supposed to. They pose no risk of flight or disappearance. They're both students and good boys. This is all a misunderstanding anyway. Nothing can be gained by forcing Mrs. Lambert to spend money she doesn't have."

His Honor frowned and said, "I see here that Tony Lambert is on probation from an earlier violation this year. This could complicate matters."

"Let's deal with it later, Your Honor. The goal right now is to get them out so they can meet with their attorney and find a solution."

Judge Pendergrast was shaking his head. "Their co-defendant, Mr. Garth Tucker, posted bail of fifty thousand dollars. This is a serious crime, Mrs. Boone."

"He's an adult and apparently his family has the money. I'm not concerned with Mr. Tucker. My clients are minors and deserve to be released from jail. There's no good reason for keeping them locked up."

Theo was sitting next to Daisy Lambert in the front row. He managed to keep a frown on his face but wanted to say, "Go get 'em, Mom!"

Judge Pendergrast said, "But for a serious charge like this, Mrs. Boone, I cannot simply release them on their personal IDs. I've never done that. And until we know the facts of this case, I cannot assume that these boys are as innocent as you think they are."

Without yielding an inch, Mrs. Boone said, "I assure you they'll show up in court when they are supposed to."

"That sounds good but I've heard it before. And, since

you will not be their lawyer after today, I'm not sure how you can guarantee anything."

"The family has little resources, Your Honor. Any type of bail will be a hardship. Indeed, any bail at all will simply keep the boys in jail. They are innocent until proven guilty."

"I realize that. Does the family own a home or any other real estate?"

Mrs. Boone exhaled in frustration and said, rather sternly, "No, Your Honor. The family rents their home. Mrs. Lambert works two jobs, one as a part-time hairstylist, the other as a waitress in a restaurant. Her husband, the boys' stepfather, works in construction and right now he's on a job two hours away. His involvement with the boys is limited. The family is barely getting by and any amount of bail is nothing but a hardship."

"For armed robbery I cannot set a bail below ten thousand dollars. For each."

"That's twenty thousand dollars, Your Honor."

"I can do the math."

"Bail bondsmen typically charge ten percent for the bond. That's two thousand dollars just to get them out. That's unfair, Your Honor."

Judge Pendergrast glared at her, obviously irritated. "Nothing I do is unfair, Mrs. Boone. I realize you do not work in criminal law, and I assure you that a ten-thousand-dollar bail for armed robbery is not unfair and is definitely on the low side. These boys got themselves in trouble. Don't blame me for it."

For a tense moment, the lawyer and the judge stared at each other, but it was obvious who was in charge. Mrs. Boone finally smiled and said, "So be it, Your Honor. Thank you for your time."

"You are welcome. Now, I have a scheduled hearing and need to move on. You are excused." In other words: Would you kindly leave my courtroom at this time?

Theo followed his mother and Daisy Lambert into the hallway where they huddled in a corner. Daisy was wiping tears and Mrs. Boone was trying to control her frustration.

Theo had almost four hundred dollars in his savings account and was already thinking of ways to get more.

"What about your husband?" Mrs. Boone asked.

"Which one?"

"The current one."

Daisy shook her head. "He won't help. We talked last night, had a big fight. He says he's not coming home for a while and will not help the boys. They've never been close."

"What about their father?"

"He's around but we don't see much of him. I'll ask him. He might pitch in something but I doubt it. He's not working much these days."

"You do that and we'll talk later. I need to get to the office and you, Theo, need to get to school."

Daisy wiped her face and said, "Thanks, Marcella. You'll never know how much I appreciate this."

"I'm not sure I helped the situation, Daisy."

"Thanks for being here. And thank you, Theo."

Theo said, "I can't believe Woody is sitting in jail."

Halfway to school, and pedaling as slowly as possible, Theo remembered that he was officially excused from class. Neither Mr. Mount nor Mrs. Gladwell nor anyone else at school would know how long things took in court, so he had a bright idea. He turned around and sprinted to the jail where he found his pal, Captain Rick Pruitt. Carrying his backpack, he explained that he needed to meet with Woody and discuss their homework. He implied that he had been sent by their teacher to help his friend keep current with their lessons.

Pruitt was skeptical and suggested that he should call the school and check out the story. Theo said that would be fine but he doubted Mrs. Gladwell would answer the phone because she was tied up in assembly.

To Theo's horror, Pruitt picked up the phone and called

the school. He asked to speak to Mrs. Gladwell, then said, "Good morning. This is Captain Pruitt at the police department. Your student, Theodore Boone, is in my office and says he needs to visit with Woody Lambert to do some homework. Was this authorized by anyone at the school?"

Theo thought about bolting, but tried to remain calm. Pruitt listened and listened, then smiled. He said, "Thanks," and hung up. He pointed at Theo and said, "If you're not in school in ten minutes, I'm calling your mother."

Theo saluted, said "Yes, sir," and ran from the office.

CHAPTER 9

Theo thought it highly unlikely that Captain Pruitt would follow up on his threat to call Mrs. Boone. It was a good bluff, and it worked because Theo was headed to school, but the closer he got the slower he pedaled. Second period was Geometry with Mrs. Garman, and it was his least-favorite subject. After a few loops and swings through the leafy neighborhoods around Stratten College, he eventually arrived at school, at precisely 10:40 when the bell rang for morning break. He checked in at the front office, went to his locker, said hello to April Finnemore, his favorite friend-girl, which was something altogether different from a real girlfriend, and drifted through the crowded hallway to Mr. Mount's classroom where Government, his favorite subject, would start at eleven o'clock.

Mr. Mount was waiting. He said softly, "Look, Theo, some of the guys are asking about Woody. What if you explained what's going on?"

Theo glanced around, obviously uncertain. He glanced at his feet, then said, "Well, sure, but I don't know how much I can say. It's a Youth Court matter and those cases are not public."

"I know. Did the judge set bail?"

"Yes, ten thousand for each. Woody's mother doesn't have the money, so they'll just stay in jail."

"That's ridiculous. Let's talk about this in class without going into the details of the armed robbery, okay?"

"Sure."

When the class was seated, Mr. Mount began with, "It's clear that Woody is absent today and missed yesterday. Some of you have asked about him, and, well, to be honest about the situation, Woody is in jail. Along with his brother Tony. Theo has been to court twice trying to help, and he knows more about what's going on. Theo."

As captain of the Debate Team, Theo had overcome his fear of speaking in public. Most of his classmates had not. Mr. Mount always said that most people, especially kids but even adults, fear public speaking. Theo enjoyed the attention, and he was secretly proud that he could do something most kids could not.

He took a deep breath and walked to the front of the class. "I just got back from Youth Court," he said gravely, as if he were the lawyer in charge of Woody's defense. "Woody is doing okay but needs to get out of jail. The facts go something like this, and I cannot reveal everything because Youth Court cases are private matters. But sometime late Tuesday night, Woody and his older brother Tony were riding around with a friend. They stopped at a convenience store, something happened, and they were arrested later for armed robbery. They appeared in court Wednesday morning and again a few hours ago. My mother is trying to help them get out. The judge set their bail at ten thousand dollars each, and the family is trying to raise the money."

"They have to raise twenty thousand dollars?" Brandon asked.

"No, not quite that much."

"What does bail mean?" Aaron asked. "I don't understand."

"It's kind of complicated," Theo replied.

Mr. Mount said, "Theo, why don't you use Woody as an example and walk us through the bail system? And keep it as simple as possible."

Theo loved moments like this when the class was stumped by a legal issue or problem. He was suddenly the smooth and gifted trial lawyer pacing in front of the jury. "Okay, so Woody got arrested, charged with a crime, and put in jail. Since he is presumed to be innocent until proven guilty, he has the right to get out of jail, regardless of the crime. But, the police need to make sure he'll show up in court when he's expected. In theory, the police need some promise that he will not run away. I think in the old days criminals just disappeared after they got out. That doesn't happen much today. Anyway, the police and judges developed the system of bail. You've heard the old saying: 'Bail him out of jail.' That's what happens. The accused is required to put up some money or some land that the court can hold to make sure he doesn't disappear. Since most people charged with crimes have little money and no property, they are forced to buy a bail bond. There are these guys who hang around the jail and the courtrooms trying to sell bail bonds to defendants. In Woody's case, his bail is ten thousand dollars. His family doesn't have that kind of money, so his mother will be forced to do business with a bail bondsman. For ten percent of the bail, in cash, this guy will give the court a bond, a written document that guarantees Woody's appearance whenever he's supposed to be in court. If Woody fails to show up, the bondsman has the right to go hunt him down and arrest him. As a rule, bail bondsmen are pretty tough guys."

"So Woody needs a thousand dollars?" Jarvis asked.

"Right. And a thousand for his brother. Their mother simply doesn't have the money, so they're still in jail. They've been there for the past two nights."

"If he's innocent, why is he stuck in jail?" asked Darren.

"Good question, and I have no good answer. Let's just say that the bail system is out of date and a lot of people are trying to change it. Last night I found online at least two national organizations working to reform bail laws. A lot of people are locked away when they should be working and taking care of their families."

"Which brings us back to Woody," Mr. Mount said. "How can we help? I guess he needs a thousand dollars."

"Not really. He needs two thousand. Mrs. Lambert has to get two boys out of jail, not just one. And Woody told her he won't leave without Tony. So it's both or nothing."

During his slow ride back to school, Theo had pondered the idea of asking his friends to chip in all the money they could find. He was ready and willing to offer his savings of four hundred dollars, but he worried that most of the others had little to offer. They were, after all, only thirteen years old. On his tenth birthday, Theo's parents had given him fifty dollars to deposit in his brand-new savings account, and each year they added fifty dollars to it. He was encouraged to stash away any spare cash he earned with the various odd jobs he was lucky enough to find. He was proud of his savings but willing to give it all away to help Woody.

Theo was luckier than most of his friends and he knew it. He was an only child of two lawyers who were watching him closely and planning his future. He was often frustrated by the high levels of supervision, but his parents always seemed to know when to back off, a little. He was taught not to compare himself to his friends, but to simply accept them for who they were.

Throwing four hundred dollars on the table like some big shot would not go over well with his friends. Chase Whipple wouldn't mind because his family had money and Theo was close to him. Brandon would be impressed by such a gesture because his goal was to be the first millionaire in the class. He had his own paper route and was trading stocks online. However, he had been complaining recently about a downturn in the market.

But the rest of the class would resent the challenge. And, it simply wouldn't work. Theo suspected that only he and two or three others had savings accounts, and he wasn't about to ask. At the moment, no one seemed eager to offer money.

Mr. Mount said, "Okay, that's our challenge. How can we raise two thousand dollars to bail out Woody and Tony?"

A nervous silence followed, with no volunteers. Finally, Jarvis asked, "Is it true that the family has no money at all?"

Theo replied, "I don't know. I'm sure Mrs. Lambert is trying to scrape together something, but I haven't asked. That's really none of my business. Woody's stepfather is working out of town and doesn't want to help."

Chase asked, "Does Woody just stay in jail forever if he can't make bail?"

"Not forever," Theo replied. "Eventually, he'll go to court to face the charges, maybe have a trial. If he's found not guilty, he'll be released. If he's found guilty, I suppose they send him away."

"Do you think he's guilty, Theo?" asked Ricardo.

"No, he's not guilty of armed robbery. We know Woody. He'd never do something as terrible as that. I've talked to him and he says it's just one big misunderstanding. He may be guilty of underage drinking, but nothing else."

Justin said, "I have a question, Theo. Suppose Woody can't bail out and has to sit in jail until his trial. How long will that take?"

"You never know. It varies, even in Youth Court. I guess several months."

"So, Woody sits in jail for months, flunks out of school,

then goes to trial and let's say he's found not guilty. He goes home right, as if nothing happened? A clean record."

"Right."

"What about the time he just served? Does he get paid for that?"

"No, of course not. It's just wasted time."

"So what's fair about this system?"

"Who said it was fair?"

"Well, you're always talking about how great the court system is, how great the law is, how much you want to be a lawyer. That's the last place I'd want to work."

Mr. Mount said, "Okay, let's get back to the issue at hand. While we're having this discussion, your friend Woody is sitting in jail, and I'm sure he is not doing his homework."

CHAPTER 10

Theo suffered through the rest of the day. During study hall, which was supervised by Mr. Mount, he was called to the principal's office. Mrs. Gladwell had prepared written instructions allowing Theo to leave an hour early and go to the jail. She had discussed Woody's situation with Judge Pendergrast and they had agreed that Theo could haul in the necessary textbooks and help his friend with his homework.

Theo knew that the last thing Woody would want to see in jail was a stack of textbooks, but he said nothing. He left the school at two p.m., an hour before final bell. With some time to spare, he detoured to the courthouse and went to the public defenders' office on the third floor where he was greeted by the same grouchy secretary he'd encountered on Tuesday.

"I'd like to see Mr. Rodney Wall," he asked without saying hello.

She stopped typing, frowned at him, and said, "It's you again. Why aren't you in school?"

"I'm excused and I have the paperwork to prove it."

She lost interest immediately, nodded toward a closed door, and said, "He's in there."

Theo knocked on the door and a squeaky voice said, "Come in."

Rodney Wall looked young enough to be a senior at Strattenburg High School. He was a small guy seated in an oversized chair that dwarfed him. He wore round glasses and a scruffy beard that was probably an effort to make up for his lack of hair. He made no effort to stand or greet his visitor.

"Can I help you?" he asked, but it was obvious that helping was not on his mind.

Theo walked to the edge of his cluttered desk and said, "Yes, I'm Theodore Boone, a friend of Woody Lambert, your client. I'd like to talk about his case."

"Oh you would?"

"Yes."

Wall arranged his hands so that his fingertips were touching. "Your mother is Marcella Boone."

"Yes."

"So is she planning to represent the Lambert boys?"

"No, she is not. She appeared this morning just to get bail set and try to get them out of jail."

"Why is she sticking her nose into my business?"

"Because you weren't there. I stopped by this place three times yesterday looking for you so we could talk about the case, and you were out of the office."

"Sometimes that happens. Sometimes lawyers need to leave their office to go out and investigate. Why aren't you in school?"

"I have an official pass from my principal, Mrs. Gladwell. Feel free to call her."

"She sent you over here to my office to quiz me about my clients?" Behind his round glasses were two small eyes that glared at Theo without blinking. He did not stop tapping his fingertips together.

"No, she sent me to the jail to help Woody with his homework. I'm on my way there now."

"I've heard about you, kid. You're always hanging around the courthouse and bugging lawyers and judges and acting like you're some kind of real lawyer. You show up in Animal Court all the time and take real cases, which anyone can do down there. Now you're here poking around in my business."

"Look, can we talk about Woody's case? He's one of my best friends and he is not guilty of armed robbery."

"No. Both of your parents are lawyers, so you should know that a lawyer cannot discuss his client's business with anyone else. It would be unethical for me to say anything about the case."

Theo knew the guy was right, and he knew he shouldn't be there sticking his nose in another lawyer's business. But he wanted Mr. Wall to know that someone was watching, and so far that someone was not too impressed with the defense. Theo asked, "Have you met with your clients yet?"

Mr. Wall gave an exaggerated sigh as if greatly frustrated. "The answer is yes, and that's the last answer I'm giving you. I met with Woody and Tony about three hours ago, and now I'm in the initial stages of writing a case report, which I will review with my supervisor and not with anyone else."

"Do you believe they're innocent?"

"Look, Mr. Theo, it's time for you to leave. I have work to do. And I suppose you need to get down to the jail and help Woody with his homework."

Theo backed away from the desk, mumbled a half-hearted "Thanks," and left the office.

Instead of going to the jail, he headed north toward the edge of town, riding ten blocks or so until he came to a strip mall. Daisy Lambert worked thirty hours a week as a hairstylist and another thirty as a waitress. Theo had never been to her salon, never had a reason to visit, and he wasn't sure he should barge right in. But the clock was ticking, in more ways than one, and now was not the time to be timid.

In the reception area, several women of all ages lounged around reading magazines with all manner of foils and rollers and clamps affixed to their hair. Beyond them two rows of chairs were filled with women getting worked on. In the rear, in the last chair, Theo saw Daisy lost in a pile of thick orange curls and clipping away. With blinders on, he walked straight toward her, ignoring everyone else along the way and said, "Hi, Mrs. Lambert, got a minute?"

Daisy was jolted at the sight of Theo in a place she would never expect him to be. "Well, sure, Theo," she said, lowering her shears. "Excuse me one moment," she whispered to her client. They stepped a few feet away and found privacy near the washing stations.

"Sorry to bother you," Theo said in a voice as low as possible.

"Something wrong?" she asked, as if she expected everything to go wrong.

"No. I'll just get right to the point. I know it's rude to talk about money but right now that's all we can talk about. I have four hundred dollars. Some of my buddies are willing to pitch in some more. I'm going to ask my parents for a loan, and maybe my uncle, Ike, too. So, how much do we need to raise?"

Her eyes watered instantly, and Theo's first thought was that he hated to see Daisy cry. She said, "Oh, Theo, you can't do this. Please."

"I'm doing it, Mrs. Lambert, okay? And I'm not going to argue. Woody is my close friend and he needs our help. Now, how much?"

She wiped her eyes, thought for a second. "I talked to his father, my ex, and he said he would try and borrow some money, but I'm not counting on it. He never comes through. I've got three hundred dollars in the bank, and I'm trying to get more out of my husband. It's tough, Theo. Times are tough for some people."

Especially Woody and Tony, he thought. "Okay, great, so we have seven hundred bucks that we can count on. That's a start. I'll get to work."

"I'll pay you back, Theo, I promise."

"I'm not worried about that right now. Have you talked to a bail bondsman?"

"No, I was going to call later this afternoon."

"I have one in mind."

"Thanks. I have to get back to work."

Theo had noticed the offices before. There were several of them on the side streets near the jail, all shady little places with cheap rents and temporary looks. They advertised with large signs, as if the guys behind bars could simply look out a window, jot down a phone number, make a call, and get out. The bail bond business seemed to attract those with backgrounds in police work and private investigations, and was not highly regulated, nor highly regarded. Theo had looked it over online and had decided he would rather not do business with any of the five companies he'd found in Strattenburg.

But, there was no other choice. Judging from the online ads, and from the looks of the office, AAA Bail Bonds seemed like the best of the bunch. He parked his bike near its front door and took a deep breath. He reminded himself that he was just a kid and most adults were not rude or insulting to kids. He also reminded himself that he had just barged into the PD's office without an appointment and stuck his nose into another lawyer's business, and he had just invaded a hair salon where he had never felt so unwelcome. This could not be as bad.

When Theo opened the door he was immediately hit with a wave of disgusting cigarette smoke. The battered reception desk was vacant. He could hear voices in the rear. Someone yelled, "Be there in a minute."

Theo waited by the door, ready to bolt if necessary. A man appeared, a thick tough-looking dude in a shirt with short sleeves that revealed biceps as round as softballs. The shirt was sort of a light orange color, which would have been fine but for the bright green tie knotted thickly at his neck. Blue jeans, pointed-toe cowboy boots, gun on the hip. He was scowling and seemed ticked off at the disturbance, but when he saw Theo he broke into a wide smile and said, "Well, what brings you here?"

"I'm Theodore Boone. My parents are Marcella and Woods Boone, both lawyers. You might know them."

"I think so. They don't do much on the criminal side, right?"

"That's right."

"So why are you here? Have a seat," he said, pointing to some plastic chairs. Theo didn't want to stay long but sat down out of courtesy. "Name's Sparky," he said.

No last name. Sparky seemed to be a fitting name for the place.

"Yes, sir, well, my friend's in jail and I'm trying to arrange his bail."

"How old is he?"

"Thirteen. Woody Lambert. He's with his brother Tony."

Sparky sat behind the desk and picked up some papers. He scanned a couple of them and said, "Oh, here it is.

Armed robbery. Ten grand each. You need for me to write the bond?"

"Sure, but the family has very little money."

"Gee, I've never heard that before. Where's the family? Why are you here?"

"The mom's working; the father is away. I'm here as a friend. Is it true that you charge ten percent for the bail bond?"

"That's the ticket, son. A thousand bucks each and I can get 'em out in no time flat. Assuming I'm convinced they're good boys with no intentions of running away."

"Why is it ten percent? Seems like it should be less when dealing with kids who aren't really capable of running away."

"Oh, you think so? What do you know about the bail bond business?"

"Not much."

"That's what I figured. Look, kid, I've been doing this for twenty years, and I can promise you that every criminal is capable of running away. They do it all the time and it's my job to go find them, grab them, bring them back here, and haul them in front of the judge. This is a risky business."

Theo could not comprehend Woody being referred to as a "criminal." He took a deep breath, uncertain about what to say next. "Is it possible to write the bond for less than ten percent?"

Sparky grunted his disapproval and waved a hand at the windows. "Not here, but feel free to go next door or across the street. But it's a waste of time. Nobody can get your friend out quicker than me. I guarantee it."

Theo hesitated and tried to look as pitiful as possible. Sparky glared at him as if they were wasting their time. Theo asked, "So, if I bring you two thousand dollars in cash, how long will it take to get them out?"

"About an hour." Sparky stood as if he suddenly had better things to do. "Now beat it, kid."

"Thanks," Theo said and walked to the door.

CHAPTER 11

At the jail, Officer Randolph examined the note from Mrs. Gladwell and told Theo to follow him. They went to a small windowless room that was barely wide enough for a narrow table and two folding chairs. Theo took a seat and unpacked his textbooks. He waited nervously, jumping at every sound in the hallway. Finally, Woody walked in and Officer Randolph closed the door behind him. It locked loudly.

Woody's left eye was swollen shut and he had a fresh cut on his forehead. He sat across from Theo and said, "You gotta get me out of here, Theo."

"What happened? You look awful."

"Got in a fight. Last night they put this guy Jock in our cell and he was serious trouble."

"What happened, Woody?"

Woody placed his hands on the table. Both were shaking. His right eye watered, and it was obvious he was a wreck. He began. "Jock is a jerk, a real bully, and a tough guy. Tony and I tried to stay away from him but the cell is not big enough. About an hour ago, when they finally brought us lunch, Jock said he wanted half of my sandwich. I said no, and I guess that was the wrong thing to say. He grabbed for the sandwich, dumped my tray, and that started it all. He was just begging for a fight. He punched me in the face, Tony jumped on his back, and Jock basically beat the crap out of us. Before the guards could get there he had us both on the floor and was kicking away. You should see Tony's face. Everybody was yelling, and when the guards grabbed Jock he yelled about how we jumped him and started it all. Two against one ain't fair and stuff like that. They took him away to another cell and the guards cussed us for starting the fight, said we'd have to spend more time in jail for fighting."

Theo was stunned. He asked, "Is Tony okay?"

"I think so. An EMT looked at him, said nothing was broken, put some ice on his face. Jock is one mean dude.

You gotta help us, Theo. We're in jail for doing nothing and this place is awful."

"I'm trying, okay? I just met with your mom and then with a bail bondsman. I also met with your lawyer, who is not that nice of a guy."

"We didn't like him at all. He started off by telling us how busy he is, how he's got fifty cases right now, all in Youth Court, and so he can't spend much time with us. We told him what happened and got the impression he didn't believe us. We need another lawyer, Theo."

"We'll worry about that later. Right now we're trying to raise bail money."

"What's that?" Woody said, nodding at the textbooks.

"Your homework. Mrs. Gladwell and Mr. Mount have decided that I need to tutor you so you won't get behind."

"I'm already behind and you can take those books back where they came from. If I wasn't doing homework at home, what makes you think I'll do it here?"

Which was a very good question and one Theo had been contemplating. Woody grimaced and pressed both hands against the sides of his head. "I don't know how many times he kicked me but my head is killing me. It's throbbing and my ears are ringing."

"Listen. We've got seven hundred dollars already. If we

get a thousand then we can bail you out and go to work on Tony's bail."

"No. I'm not leaving here without him. It's both of us or nothing."

"Come on, Woody. You're thirteen, he's sixteen. He can survive here longer than you."

"Oh really? You should see him now, see how well he's surviving. I'm not leaving without Tony."

Theo shook his head. "Okay, okay."

Nothing was said for a long minute. Woody gently massaged his temples as he frowned and closed his eyes. Theo felt like crying, but not here. This was jail and everybody played the tough guy.

"What's everybody saying about me?" Woody asked. "I'm sure the whole school knows I'm in jail."

"I haven't talked to the whole school. Our gang knows what's going on and everyone is on your side. You've done nothing wrong and all your buddies are trying to get you out. Mr. Mount is concerned and wants to help. Mrs. Gladwell has talked to the judge. We're with you, Woody."

Woody took a deep breath and managed a smile, as if relieved.

Theo said, "Don't worry about everybody else, Woody. Only your friends matter and we're all on your side."

"That stupid kid Garth. I wish Jock could go a round or two with him."

Theo slowly put the textbooks into his backpack. "You're not leaving, are you?" Woody asked. "What's the hurry?"

"No. I won't leave until they make me."

They chatted for almost an hour and Theo managed to get a couple of laughs out of his friend. Officer Randolph tapped on the door and said time was up.

At the front desk, Theo picked up his cell phone and checked his messages. Mr. Mount texted that he had two hundred dollars for the cause. Chase was calling a meeting of the gang at Guff's Yogurt for four thirty.

Theo hopped on his bike and raced to the shabby old office where his uncle Ike worked occasionally. Ike was the older brother of Woods Boone and had once been a prominent lawyer in town. But he encountered some sort of vague "trouble" and was forced to leave the profession. He spent a few months in jail, long before Theo was born. Ike never talked about what happened, nor did Theo's parents.

His office was on the second floor of an old building owned by a Greek family that ran a deli downstairs. Theo hustled up the stairs, barged into the office, and found Ike at his desk, buried in paperwork, sipping a late afternoon beer, and listening to the Grateful Dead on the stereo. "What's this?" he growled. He adored his only nephew but didn't like the surprise intrusion.

Theo stopped by every Monday afternoon for a required visit, but never on Thursdays. He blurted, "Ike, I need to borrow some money."

"I don't have any money, Theo. What's going on?"

"Okay, I'll be brief. One of my good friends is in jail and I'm trying to bail him out. His family has no money for bail and I'm trying to round up two thousand dollars. I'm putting up all of my savings, all four hundred dollars."

"Must be a real good friend. Why was he arrested?"

"Armed robbery. It's a long story but he's not guilty."

"Don't they all say that? A kid charged with armed robbery?"

"Look, Ike, I'll explain it all later. Right now I need some money. I've never asked you before and I'll never ask you again. And it's a loan. I promise I'll pay it back. One day. Somehow."

Ike scratched his beard and pulled at his gray ponytail. "Pretty serious aren't you?"

"Dead serious, Ike."

"How do you plan to pay it back? You're not exactly employed yet."

"I'll think of something. Trust me."

Ike studied him for a long time and began to smile. Slowly, he reached into a drawer, removed a three-ring checkbook, and scribbled something. He tore out the check and handed it over. "Two hundred dollars. It's the best I can do. And it's a loan, not a gift."

Theo snatched the check, said, "You're the greatest, Ike," and took off.

As Theo climbed onto his bike, his phone buzzed. It was a text from Daisy. Woody's father had somehow found $100. Their effort was now at $1,200, enough to spring Woody.

Theo texted Elsa at the office and explained that he was helping Woody with his homework and would be running by the office. He was expected to stop there every afternoon, check in with Elsa and his parents, and hit the homework. At thirteen, he was growing tired of this ritual and longed for a bit of freedom. Next year he would enter the ninth grade, and high school, and he often wondered how his routine might change. Surely his parents would relax a little and give him some space.

But on the other hand, Theo loved being thirteen and an eighth grader. He and his buddies were the big dudes on campus and the younger students looked up to them. He had heard stories of ninth-grade boys and how they were ignored in high school, especially by the ninth-grade girls who became infatuated with older guys.

He pondered these things as he headed downtown. He also continued the debate about asking his parents for a loan. He knew they would freak out when he told them he was handing over his savings for Woody's bail. That would be an ugly fight but he was determined to follow through. Once that discussion was over, he doubted they would be willing to contribute more. Though he admired his mother for showing up in court that morning, last night's family argument was still fresh. He was right and they were wrong, but he didn't have the stomach for more fighting.

Of Theo's inner circle of friends, Chase Whipple was the kid who spent more time online than anyone else and could perform magic with a computer. For fun, he often wrote his own software and seemed able to find anything on the Internet in a matter of seconds. His parents were affluent and bought him the latest devices and gadgets and he was always one step ahead of the others in the high-tech race.

The gang—Chase, Aaron, Brian, Edward, and Joey—were in the rear of Guff's Frozen Yogurt huddled around a table. Theo got a small vanilla with cookie dough and joined them. "What's the latest?" Chase asked.

"We're at twelve hundred dollars," Theo reported. "Four

hundred from me, three hundred from Woody's mother, one hundred from his father, two hundred from Mr. Mount, and I just got a check for two hundred from Ike, a loan."

"You're putting up four hundred dollars?" Aaron asked in disbelief.

"Yep, all my savings."

"That's awesome, Theo."

"Wish I had more. I just spent an hour with Woody and he got beat up today. Big black eye, a cut. Some dude jumped him in jail. We gotta work fast, guys."

"I have a hundred in savings," Aaron said.

"Me too," said Joey.

"I'm still looking," said Brian.

"That's great. Fourteen hundred."

"Isn't that enough to get him out?" asked Brian.

Theo said, "Yes, but that's not the deal, remember? Woody won't leave without Tony, so we need two thousand dollars, like I said."

"I'm broke," Chase said, "but here's the plan. Ever hear of MobMoney?"

"No," Theo replied. The others shook their heads.

Chase had the floor and said, "MobMoney is one of the latest crowdfunding schemes, but it's primarily for kids. I found it this afternoon and I've been working on it. Take a look." He opened his laptop and the boys squeezed behind him.

"Sounds like the Mafia or something," Edward said.

"That's because you watch too many old movies," Chase said. "This has nothing to do with crime and is strictly legit. It works like this." He pecked a few keys and a photo of Woody was on the screen. Below it was the caption: "Woody Lambert, Age 13, In jail for a crime he didn't commit." Below the caption was a drawing of a kid sitting on a bunk in a jail cell with his hands cuffed, head hanging low. Below was the narrative:

> Imagine being arrested and falsely charged with a serious crime, armed robbery, and not having enough money to post bail and get out to prove your innocence. That's what's happening to Woody Lambert, age 13, of Strattenburg. He sits in jail, another victim of a system in serious need of bail reform. We, his friends, urge you to pledge any amount to FREE WOODY.

"This looks awesome, Chase," Brian said. "How does it work?"

"It's simple. If you guys approve, I click here at the bottom, and this page is instantly posted on the MobMoney website. If all goes well, the cash starts pouring in from all over the country."

"You really think we can raise enough?" Joey asked.

"I have no idea but there's nothing to lose," Chase said. "MobMoney gets ten percent, same as the other crowdfunding sites, and it sends the rest to us."

"Let's do it," Aaron said.

Chase looked at Theo and asked, "Should we run it by Woody, or maybe his mother?"

Without hesitating, Theo said, "No. Right now they'll do anything to get him out. I say we go for it."

The others agreed, and Chase clicked on *Submit.* "Done. We're in business. You can go to the website at any time and monitor the donations. Maybe we'll get lucky." He closed the laptop and took a bite of yogurt.

The boys relaxed around the table.

"Tell us about the fight, Theo," Brian said.

Theo relayed the details as given by Woody, without embellishment, and ended with, "There might be some more trouble. Woody said one of the deputies, when they broke up the fight, blamed Woody and Tony for starting it, and said they would have to spend more time in jail."

"Can they do that?" Joey asked.

"I'm not sure. Let's worry about that later."

CHAPTER 12

Woody's new cell was a damp, dark little pit with barely enough heat to knock off the chill and a small yellowish bulb hanging from the ceiling to create shadows. There was a cot with one thin, dirty blanket, a chair, a commode, and a sink. There was no cell mate because there was not enough room for one. The walls were all cinder block, painted what appeared to be a dull dark gray, and no windows. The door was metal with a small window. He was alone, with no idea where Tony had been taken, no idea who was next door or across the hall. He could hear nothing but the distant hum of some type of motor or engine.

After an hour in solitary confinement, he started thinking of how nice it would be if Theo had left behind those dreaded textbooks, along with a pen and something to write on.

The cot squeaked when he stretched out and stared at the yellow lightbulb above, too far to reach. Sleep would be a welcome relief. Sleep would take him away from this mess and perhaps a dream would take him to a beach or the mountains. He had seen news stories of innocent men released from prison after serving decades, but he had never really stopped to feel sorry for them. He figured they must have done something wrong. And here he was, stuck in a jail as the hours and days crept by, a thoroughly innocent kid wasting time behind bars. Did anybody feel sorry for him? He was comforted to know that Theo and his friends were scrambling around trying to raise bail money, but two thousand dollars seemed impossible.

He thought of his father, a man who'd had a hard life and had made bad decisions that only compounded his problems. Where was he while two of his sons were in jail? And his stepfather? Why couldn't he do something bold for a change and help the family?

Woody swore revenge against both men.

He rubbed the sore knots on his scalp and thought about

Jock. Surely these idiot deputies had thrown that little thug into solitary as well. He provoked the fight then screamed like the victim. He worried about Tony, whose face was a mess. Surely they had taken him to see a doctor. He thought about his poor mother out there frantically trying to raise money.

And he thought about the future. The shock of being accused and arrested was wearing off, and a grim and frightening reality was settling in. At first Woody assumed that the misunderstanding would be cleared up in a matter of hours and he would go home. The system would deal with Garth, the guilty one. But as time was passing behind bars, Woody was beginning to fear the system. If they could convict an innocent man of murder and lock him away for thirty years, then they could just as easily send Woody and Tony away for a few months. Their lawyer, Mr. Rodney Wall, did not inspire a lot of confidence. He seemed to doubt their stories.

A hard knock on the door jolted him. It opened in and a deputy stepped in and handed him dinner on a plastic tray. Another deputy stood guard at the door, as if Woody might jump the first one, grab his gun, and start a jailbreak.

When they were gone, Woody sat on the cot with the tray balanced on his knees. A peanut butter sandwich on stale white bread, some sad little chunks of fruit in a cup, an apple, two slices of cheddar cheese, and a small carton of mango juice. He picked up the carton and stared at it. Mango juice? He was almost certain that he had never tasted such a beverage.

He choked it all down because he was hungry, and because there was nothing else to do. When he finished, he placed the tray on the floor and stretched out on the cot. He stared at the yellow bulb until he fell asleep.

A half a mile away, Theo was at his desk in the rear of Boone & Boone, with his dog at his feet and his homework spread before him, but he wasn't studying. He and Chase and the others had agreed to hit social media hard and drum up support for Woody. They passed along to everyone they knew the scheme of flooding MobMoney with donations, but things were off to a slow start. By seven p.m. Thursday, only forty-one dollars had been raised.

Because Mrs. Boone was a busy woman who didn't like to cook, the family dined out almost every night. And they had their rituals. Thursday dinner was always roasted chicken at a Turkish deli, with spicy hummus and pita bread. Theo biked over and met his parents, who came from the office.

The situation was still a bit tense, and it didn't improve when Theo informed his parents that he was pledging his entire savings to spring Woody from jail. They didn't like it, but at the same time they grudgingly admired his loyalty. The deli was busy so they spoke in low voices.

"It has taken you a long time to save that money," his father said with a frown. Theo knew that. After all, he was the one who had saved the money. Why did adults always say things that were so obvious?

"I'll start saving again," Theo said. "The money is just sitting there in the bank, doing nothing. Might as well put it to good use. Some of the other guys are doing the same thing."

"And how much is Daisy contributing?" his mother asked.

"She doesn't have any money, Mom. We've had this conversation. She says she has only three hundred dollars in the bank. Mind if I check something?"

He asked this as he pulled out his cell phone, which was against the family rules at dinner. His parents thought it was really bad manners to stare at a cell phone during a meal. "We're up to seventy-five dollars," Theo said, and then explained the scheme behind MobMoney. His parents had never heard of crowdfunding.

Mrs. Boone and Mr. Boone exchanged the kind of adult look that kids are not supposed to understand. She said, "I suppose our law firm could help out a little. Don't you think so, Woods?"

"Well, sure. How much are you thinking?"

"How about two-fifty, Theo?"

"That's great," he said, but it wasn't great at all. If he, an unemployed thirteen-year-old, could pledge four hundred, then why couldn't his parents, both busy and successful lawyers, donate a lot more than two-fifty?

"So what's the total now?" his mother asked.

Theo mentally added the numbers and said, "Over seventeen hundred. We're getting close."

Theo checked the website before he fell asleep just after eleven. Money was trickling in from around the country, and it was adding up. Almost three hundred had been pledged to Free Woody!

Seven hours later, Theo was wide awake and staring at the screen of his laptop. MobMoney was over five hundred dollars, more than enough to spring Woody and Tony. He ran downstairs and informed his mother, and he insisted he be allowed to skip school to arrange the bail.

She agreed to write a note permitting him to arrive two hours late.

Theo called Daisy with the news, and they worked out a plan to collect all the money that had been promised. He called Mr. Mount at home and said he would be late for school, but planned to show up with Woody. He texted his friends and ordered them to round up all the cash they could find. Chase shut down the MobMoney account and was collecting the money, which would take a few hours. At nine a.m. sharp he walked into the lobby of the bank on Main Street and politely asked a teller to empty his savings account. His father had assured him it was a simple transaction, but it took half an hour anyway. He left the bank with a cashier's check for $402, all of his savings, but he didn't care. He was only thirteen. He was somewhat proud of the fact that he could use his money to help a friend, plus he could start saving all over again. And what good was a savings account for a kid like him? He was an only child whose parents would one day happily pay for his college and anything else he needed. Besides, there was always the chance that Woody would pay him back.

He went to Boone & Boone and enlisted the help of Elsa. With his check and the ones from Ike and his parents, the total was $852. Daisy arrived with $500 in cash. She had managed to borrow some from friends. At school, Mr. Mount had $400—his pledge plus another $200 from Aaron and Joey. He and Chase were attempting to collect from the MobMoney site.

"What's a wire transfer?" Theo asked Elsa.

"It's a way of moving money quickly. Banks do it all the time. One bank simply wires money to another, electronically, and they skip the hassle of mailing checks."

"So how long will it take to get the MobMoney?"

"Not sure, but it shouldn't take long. A few hours."

"Where do they send the money?" Daisy asked.

They were sitting in the large conference room on the first floor, just down the hall from Mrs. Boone's office. It was Theo's favorite room, with a long wide table and thick leather chairs all around. The walls were covered with old, heavy law books that were seldom used. Daisy sipped coffee and looked as though she hadn't slept in a week.

Elsa said, "Well, I suppose we could use our trust account, Boone & Boone."

"What's a trust account?" Theo asked.

"Every law firm has a bank account that's used to hold money that belongs to clients. It's called a trust account. The money does not belong to the lawyers but they hold it in trust for their clients. Pretty routine stuff. I'll check with Mrs. Boone."

Theo said, "I guess we should call their lawyer to make sure he knows what's going on."

Daisy said, "I called him an hour ago but he's in court. I left a message but he never calls back."

"Not sure about that guy," Theo said.

"He's always talking about how busy he is."

"Don't all lawyers do that?" Elsa said, then quickly changed the subject with, "What about the bail bondsman? Have you talked to him?"

"No, I haven't," Daisy said.

"I'll go see him," Theo said.

"You need to go to school, young man," Elsa said.

"I'm too busy for school."

Elsa peered over her reading glasses and gave him a look he had seen many times. "Shall I have a chat with Mrs. Boone?"

Theo stood slowly and headed for the door. "Don't do that. I'll stop by and see the guy on my way."

"Thanks again, Theo," Daisy said.

"They're not out yet," he said as he left.

Sparky was not to be found at AAA Bail Bonds. Theo spoke to a secretary, who asked why he wasn't in school, and asked her to get Sparky to call him. She said sure but seemed preoccupied with other matters.

Reluctantly, he biked, as slowly as possible, across town to Strattenburg Middle School, knowing that the next few hours would be a waste of time. The clock was ticking and he worried that if Woody and Tony were not released on that Friday afternoon, things might get complicated over the weekend.

CHAPTER 13

The wire transfer from MobMoney did not arrive until four p.m. Friday afternoon. Theo was sitting in the conference room, waiting. He had deposited all the cash and checks, a total of $1752, into the Boone & Boone trust account, with his mother's approval, and when the wire landed there was a total of $2320. They would worry about the excess funds later.

Since Mrs. Boone would write the checks from the firm's trust account, she agreed to call AAA Bail Bonds and get the details. She was informed that Sparky was out of town and there was no one else available to write the bond. She called Rodney Wall's office to request his assistance, but was informed that he had left for the day. His cell phone went straight to voice mail. She called another bail bond company, Action Bonds, and was encouraged when a Mr. Bob Hawley agreed to see her. She and Theo left immediately and drove to Action's office, also near the courthouse. Daisy was at work at the salon and could not get off.

Action did business from a grungy little room just down the street from AAA. Bob Hawley inspired all the confidence of a man who sold used cars, but at least he was pleasant and seemed eager to help. He pulled out some forms, took a few notes, and called the jail.

His smile vanished and he frowned as he listened. When he rang off he said, "Sorry, but there's some bad news. Seems as though the boys can't get out right now."

"And why not?" Mrs. Boone demanded.

"They put a hold on them. There was a fight or some kind of trouble at the jail, so now they're locked down in solitary confinement."

"That's ridiculous," Theo blurted. "Another dude jumped them. It wasn't their fault."

Hawley shrugged as if he heard this all the time. "Can't help it, son. You'll have to talk to the judge."

Mrs. Boone glanced at her watch and said, "It's four thirty on Friday afternoon. I'm sure the judge has already left."

Another shrug.

Theo whipped out his cell phone and speed-dialed

Judge Frank Pendergrast's office. Voice mail, closed for the weekend, call back Monday.

They thanked Mr. Hawley, left, and walked two blocks to the jail where Theo led his mother straight to the desk of Captain Rick Pruitt, her former client. Pruitt was certainly not expecting to see Mrs. Boone at the jail but was clearly impressed by her presence. She explained their predicament and Pruitt immediately grabbed a file to review the matter.

He led them to a reception area and they waited as he flipped through the pages, his frown getting heavier with each paragraph. Finally, he said, "Yep, looks like there was a disturbance of some sort in the jail and the Lambert boys are in a bit of hot water, not to mention that armed robbery. The jail reported to Youth Court and Judge Pendergrast put a hold on their release pending further orders."

"I don't understand," Mrs. Boone said.

"Happens all the time back there, Mrs. Boone. We can't have the inmates fighting among themselves so we take a hard line on bad behavior."

"It wasn't his fault," Theo said. "He and Tony got jumped by another dude."

Mrs. Boone asked, "If I can find Judge Pendergrast, can he release the hold over the weekend?"

"He's a judge, ma'am, and they usually do whatever they want. But you're calling him over the weekend?"

"Oh, I've done it before, not Pendergrast, but plenty of other judges."

"I'll help any way I can," Pruitt said.

"Thanks."

Half an hour later, Theo returned to the jail with text-books and workbooks stuffed into his heavy backpack. By now he felt like a regular, and the deputies and jailers and secretaries were no longer amused by the sight of a kid visiting the place and walking around as if he practically owned it. He spoke to them all, called them by name, was very polite because he had learned the valuable lesson years earlier that adults are always impressed by kids who are polite.

After twenty-four hours in solitary, Woody's face had improved little. His left eye was still puffy and practically closed. The cut on his forehead had scabbed over and there was swelling around it. He seemed calm, though, and not as nervous as the day before. He described the dark little dungeon where they kept him, and the terrible food, and the boredom. He had no idea where Tony was but had heard from a guard that Jock had been released Friday morning.

"Think about that, Theo," he said. "Garth pulls a stupid stunt, gets us arrested, and he's been out since Wednesday morning. Then we get attacked by a pit bull named Jock and we get the blame. He gets out, too. We're completely innocent but we're still here. This system ain't working too well, Theo."

"I know, but we're trying, Woody. We've raised the money and my mom tried to sign the paperwork an hour ago. Now she's trying to find the judge, but it might be Monday."

"Monday? Come on, Theo, I can't stay here all weekend."

"We're trying, Woody. That's all we can do."

Woody's shoulders slumped in defeat.

Friday dinner was always at Malouf's, an old restaurant owned by a Lebanese couple. Theo complained to his mother that he was not feeling well and begged off. Plus, he thought his parents might enjoy an evening to themselves. The family had had a rough week, and he really wanted some time away from his parents.

The truth was that Theo disliked the idea of eating in a nice restaurant while his friend was stuck in a dungeon, choking down bad food. Mrs. Boone had been unable to locate Judge Pendergrast, so posting bail was not possible. Theo was furious at the system, and the way that the judges and policemen, even the lawyers, seemed to think that staying in jail a few more days was no big deal.

After another awful meal of vanilla wafers and not one but two cheese sandwiches, Woody was relaxing on his bed and trying to stay warm when a sudden knock jolted him to his feet. A guard walked in, said get up and follow me, and Woody did as ordered. With no handcuffs, he was led upstairs to the main wing, down a familiar hallway, and shown to a cell where Tony was waiting.

Their solitary confinement days were over. The cell was nicer and warmer, with two bunk beds and a small shelf with half a dozen paperbacks strewn about.

Sitting side by side on the bottom bunk, and talking in low voices, they compared notes and wounds. The cuts and bruises were healing slowly. Tony had heard that Jock was gone, thank goodness, so perhaps they were somewhat safer. Woody described his meeting with Theo and delivered the welcome news that the bail money had been raised. However, they would not be released until Monday.

"How did Theo find two thousand dollars?" Tony asked.

"Everybody pitched in. Mom, Theo, the Boones, my friends, a teacher, lots of folks. Even Dad came through with some money."

"Dad?"

"Yep. Hard to believe. Theo said Garth is having a fine time on Facebook, laughing about his big adventure and bragging about what his lawyer will do. What a creep."

"And he's been out since Wednesday morning. Go figure. I might punch that jerk when I see him."

They entertained that pleasant thought for a moment, then Woody said, "I can't believe it but I kinda missed this cell. They had me in a dungeon."

"Me too. We gotta get outta here, Woody. I'm not cut out for jail. Been doing a lot of thinking lately and I might just pick up my game a little, go back to class, hit the books, get serious about the future."

"Same thoughts here. I've been thinking about Mom and how hard her life is. And we're not making things any easier. The least we can do is straighten up and stay in school."

"And avoid stupid mistakes. You know, Woody, nothing good happens when you're riding around at night, on a school night even, drinking beer. It was pretty stupid, and I want to say I'm sorry. We had no business running around with Garth, and I feel bad because I forced you to do it. I'm your big brother and I'm supposed to set a good example. I blew it. My bad, kid."

Tony put an arm around Woody's shoulders and squeezed him. "It won't happen again."

Woody didn't like being hugged by his brother but he was touched by his apology. "It's not your fault, Tony. We knew what we were doing."

"You're only thirteen, and every kid your age is influenced by older people, especially family members. I blew it, and I promise it won't happen again." Tony removed his arm and Woody relaxed.

"Thanks," he said. "I'm just glad we're together again."

"Right, and we're going to stick together. We did nothing wrong and we can't let Garth and his lawyer trick us into a bad deal. Got it?"

"Whatever you say."

CHAPTER 14

Early Saturday morning, Judge Frank Pendergrast was snoozing in his recliner in the den, still in his pajamas. It had been another long night with little sleep. For about the tenth night in a row, his bloodhound had gone berserk around midnight, barking and howling and lunging at the kitchen door. Once again, he had stepped outside onto the patio and listened in disbelief as every dog on the street yelped and shrieked hysterically in one endless chorus. Something was provoking the neighborhood dogs to go nuts at midnight, and once the racket started it went on for hours. He had talked to his neighbors and no one was sleeping. No one had ever seen their dogs behave in such a bizarre manner. It was like a ghost was running door-to-door and whipping the animals into a frenzy. Something had to be done, but what? How do you catch a ghost?

Just as he dozed off again, the phone rang and he grabbed for it. A mistake.

A familiar voice said, "Good morning, Frank, this is Marcella Boone. Hate to bother you at home but this is important. Hope I didn't disturb."

Oh no, Marcella. It's only Saturday morning, my day off, and I haven't slept in days. And you called me "Frank" as opposed to "Judge Pendergrast."

He swallowed hard and said, "Well, good morning, Marcella. To what do I owe this honor?" He asked the question but he had a hunch.

"It's the Lambert boys, Frank. They're still in jail. We've raised the money for their bail and tried to get them out yesterday afternoon. However, there is a hold on them because of a fight at the jail. They can't get out until Monday, which is outrageous."

The tone of her voice left little doubt that Marcella believed strongly in her cause and was itching for a fight. He had always admired her, and Woods as well, and he really didn't want trouble. For the most part, the local bar—the lawyers and judges—knew one another well and strived to get along. There was nothing to be gained by fighting and bickering, regardless of the conflicts they dealt with. It was a civilized bar and they took pride in their professionalism.

He stood, scratched his head, and said, "Well, I'm not sure what's happening here, Marcella. I do not recall hearing anything about a fight."

"The jailers are blaming you. They told us you are reprimanding the boys for fighting in jail. Is this true?"

"No, it is not. This is the first I've heard about it. I'm not sure what's going on."

"Listen, Frank, this is what's going on. The Lambert boys were arrested Tuesday night and charged with armed robbery. The guy with the gun, and the driver of the car, posted bail Wednesday morning and is having his fun on social media. His family has money. The Lamberts do not. Once in jail, they were attacked by another juvenile named Jock. I'm sure you know of him, and he's already out. We have managed to beg and borrow the money necessary to post bail, ten thousand dollars each, which, in my opinion, is excessive, but nonetheless we have the money and we want the boys out. Now."

Had they been in the courtroom, His Honor would consider gently suggesting that Mrs. Boone relax her tone a bit. He felt as though he was being reprimanded. But the courtroom was far away, and he was standing in the middle of his den, in his pajamas, and he felt all of his power draining away.

He said, "Marcella, I swear I do not remember anything about a fight."

"I'm not surprised. That jail is a zoo and you know how often the paperwork gets lost. May I suggest you call down there and instruct them to get the boys ready to be released? I've just talked to the bail bondsman and he can meet us at the jail in an hour. As I said, Frank, we have the money."

It was such a silly fight, and a small one. And he knew she was not going away. His Honor really wanted to crawl back into his recliner, snuggle under his quilt, and try to resume his nap. "Sure, Marcella."

"Thank you, Frank. And tell Caroline I'll see her at the luncheon next Wednesday."

"Will do."

An hour later, Theo and his mother met Daisy Lambert at the jail. Mr. Bob Hawley of Action Bail Bonds arrived on time and was all smiles. Mrs. Boone wrote two one thousand dollar checks from the firm's trust account, and Daisy signed the necessary paperwork. It took another hour to round up the Lambert boys. They were given their cell phones and personal effects, then handed over to their mother. When they walked outside, they stopped and took a long, deep breath of fresh air, and soaked up the sunshine. After a round of hugs and thank-yous, Woody and Tony hopped in the car with Daisy and sped away.

As Theo and his mother watched them disappear, he said, "Well, that was easy."

The last thing Woody had in mind for his first full afternoon of freedom, and a Saturday no less, was to slog his way through a pile of homework. However, he had no choice. Pursuant to an agreement hammered out by his mother, Mr. Mount, Mrs. Gladwell, and Theo, he dutifully reported to Strattenburg Middle at two p.m. for an intense study session.

When he arrived, Woody admitted, but only to himself, that he had actually missed the place. He met Theo and Mr. Mount in their empty homeroom and was glad to see them. They spent half an hour talking about his days in jail, and Woody quickly grew to enjoy his own stories. There were some laughs, and for the moment his legal troubles were somewhere else. Under Mr. Mount's guidance, they studied for three straight hours.

That night, the gang surrounded Woody. Theo, Chase, Brian, Justin, Ricardo, and Aaron met him at Guff's for a frozen yogurt, then they walked to the downtown cinema and watched Spider-Man 7. By ten, Woody was back home watching late night TV with his mother and Tony, eating popcorn and laughing about how much they missed Jock.

CHAPTER 15

By Monday morning, the entire eighth grade knew that Woody was free and returning to school. To avoid attention, he arrived early and secured himself in homeroom with Mr. Mount. His facial wounds were still visible and he was tired of talking about them. On the one hand, he was embarrassed by his arrest and legal troubles, but on the other hand he was thrilled to be back at school with his buddies. And if the girls wanted to smile and say hello, that was okay, too. Several times during the morning, as he was once again welcomed back, he said, "Yeah, Theo got me out."

Theo wanted no credit whatsoever. He had helped a friend in need, something he would readily do again. He was delighted to see Woody smiling. They had hit the books hard over the weekend and Woody seemed eager to catch up. Their teachers—Madame Monique in Spanish, Miss Garman in Geometry, Mr. Tubcheck in Chemistry, and, of course Mr. Mount in Government—acted as though Woody had never missed a class. Each quietly offered to meet with him after school for extra tutoring.

At lunch, Theo and April Finnemore bought a sandwich and sat together on the playground, alone. They had not spoken much in the past days. Theo had been so preoccupied with Woody's bail that he had neglected her. April was a quiet, shy girl from a troubled family and she needed Theo's attention. She was different, a loner who enjoyed reading and painting. Her style of dress was whispered to be "artsy," and she cut her hair short. She had few girlfriends and didn't want any. The other girls were too busy staring at their phones, gossiping about one another, and April considered them to be "airheads."

"Did you really get him out, Theo?" she asked.

Theo rarely bragged. His parents had taught him to be humble and let his actions speak for themselves. Nobody likes a braggart, his father had said many times, especially around the golf course where big talking was not unusual.

But with April, Theo felt secure. She would never repeat anything. So he took a deep breath and replayed the entire story.

Monday afternoon brought the required visit to see Uncle Ike. Theo had mixed feelings about it because Ike was generally in a foul mood and had nothing good to say about anything or anybody. He was a lonely old man with few friends and no family. His wife divorced him long ago when he went to prison and his adult children were far away and too busy to call. But as Theo grew older, he began to wonder if Ike was as unhappy as he let on. He played poker at least once a week with a group of retired lawyers and cops. He knew more courthouse gossip than anyone. He was in a weird book club that read only biographies. Elsa had once dropped a hint that Ike had a longtime lady friend in another town. Theo suspected that being grumpy was just part of Ike's routine.

"How's my favorite nephew?" he asked as Theo fell into the creaky leather chair. Judge settled next to his feet. Same question every Monday.

"I'm your only nephew. My buddy got out. Thanks for the loan."

"Don't mention it. How's he doing?"

"He came back to school today and was like a hero. You want to hear about his armed robbery?"

"Sure." Ike wheeled around his swivel chair, reached into a small fridge, removed a can of beer and a can of ginger ale.

He turned a knob on his stereo and lowered the volume so that Bob Dylan could barely be heard. He popped the top and swung his feet onto his desk. Same old sandals.

Theo described the armed robbery with the water pistol. When he finished he asked, "What will happen to Woody?"

"He'll probably get the death penalty in this town."

"Come on, Ike. They can't convict him of anything, can they?"

"Does he have a good lawyer?"

"Public defender."

"Some of those guys are good. I don't know much about Youth Court, Theo. I was far away from my youth when I got busted."

"Plus, you were a tax lawyer, right?"

"Right. I stayed away from the criminal stuff, that is, until they came after me. How are your grades?"

"Perfect," Theo said immediately. He had learned that anything less than straight A's would prompt a mini-lecture on the virtues of studying harder. How many adults were carefully watching his grades? Too many.

Ike took a swig of beer and asked, "How are things over at Boone and Boone?"

"The same. Everybody's working too hard." Ike had been a partner with Theo's parents before he was born.

"And your mother?"

"She's fine." Ike never asked about Woods Boone, his brother. "Can I ask you a question, Ike, something that might be sort of off-limits?"

"Maybe. What's it about?"

"A long time ago you got into trouble."

"It's not something I talk about. I might explain things one day when you're older, maybe not."

"Okay. I'm not asking about what you did wrong, if anything. My question is this: Did you have to post bail to get out of jail?"

Ike took another drink and studied the ceiling fan for a long time. Theo was suddenly worried that he had ventured into forbidden territory.

Ike said, "My situation was different. I knew the police wanted me, so I went with my lawyer down to the station. I was photographed and fingerprinted, all that jazz, and placed in a cell for about an hour. Then I was released on personal identification. So, no, I wasn't forced to make bail."

"Bail seems so unfair. I found an article about it online. This legal scholar wrote that people with no money get stuck in jail for crimes that are not that serious. Shoplifting, bad checks, small drug cases, expired driver's licenses, stuff like that. This is while they are presumed to be innocent and long before they go to court. A lot of men lose their jobs and a lot of mothers are separated from their children just because they can't make bail."

"He's right about that. It's been a problem for a long time. Did this scholar offer a solution?"

"It's pretty obvious. Cut out bail for small crimes and let people go home. He says that virtually all of them will show up for court anyway. Keep bail in place for those charged with violent and serious crimes."

"And you like to read stuff like this?"

"Yes I do."

"Most kids your age are reading comic books or playing video games, and you're reading about problems with our legal system." Ike was amused and took another sip of his beer.

"Yes, and the more I read the more problems I find."

"Our legal system is pretty good, Theo, better than most, but it could work much more efficiently if we would fix the problems."

"Bail reform, long prison sentences for nonviolent guys, mass incarceration, wrongful convictions, electing judges. I'm finding all kinds of stuff about how messed up our system really is. It's depressing, Ike, especially for a kid who wants to be a lawyer."

"So, what are you going to do about it?"

"I don't know. I'm only thirteen and my parents will not let me go to law school until I finish college."

"Sounds cruel to me."

"Worse than cruel. So, I suppose I'll just keep reading about the problems until I'm old enough to do something about them."

"Who says you have to wait? Take Woody's case. Watch what happens to him. Study our Youth Court system and you'll find plenty of problems. I'm told that our juvenile prisons are in really bad shape. We're talking kids here, Theo, youngsters like you, so why not get involved to improve things? I'll bet you can find several groups active in Youth Court reform."

"I've already run across a couple."

"There you go. Get involved now. Don't wait ten years. The problems are just getting worse."

Theo sipped his ginger ale and absorbed Ike's words. "I don't know. I'm pretty busy right now."

"You sound like your parents. Not happy unless they're talking about being so busy. You're thirteen, Theo, not forty. Don't fall into the trap of planning every moment of every day and keeping an eye on the clock. You know who John Lennon was, right?"

"The Beatle?"

"That's him. In his lyrics he said a lot of wise things. One

I remember goes something like this: 'Life is what happens to you while you're busy making other plans.' Get it?"

"I guess."

"If you see a problem, Theo, think of a way to fix it and do it now. Don't spend all your time making plans."

"What are you trying to fix, Ike?"

"Nothing. I don't see any problems, plus I'm too old. Now beat it so I can finish this pile of paperwork."

"See you next Monday."

CHAPTER 16

On Tuesday morning, Theo stood in front of his locker with a looming sense of dread. He was tired because he'd stayed up the night before reading legal articles on America's broken bail system. The more he read the more frustrated he became and he couldn't go to sleep. Sometime after midnight he finally dozed off, with his laptop still open.

A soft voice behind him said, "Um, Theo."

He turned and found a slight, dark-haired boy he didn't know. The kid was immediately uncomfortable, switching his weight back and forth as he struggled to find words, and glancing around. He was either frightened or intimidated.

"What's up?" Theo said. He recognized the boy as a seventh grader but did not know his name. He was holding a piece of paper that at first glance did not appear to be anything related to schoolwork.

"I'm Roger, and the police gave this to my mother last night before they took him." He sort of shoved the paper at Theo, who took it and with one glance recognized the problem.

"A Rule Three Summons," Theo said. "For Animal Court."

Roger said, "I hear you're good at handling these cases."

"What's the name of the defendant? I'm having trouble reading this."

"Rufus, our pet rabbit. He's a French Lop."

Okay, thought Theo. In his Animal Court career, he had been involved with two dogs, including Judge, a spitting llama, fainting goats, a delinquent parrot, and an otter that feasted off fat goldfish. But never a lop-eared rabbit. "Says here the infraction is for a 'recurring nightly disturbance.' Any idea what that might be?"

"No clue. Our family lets Rufus roam free in the house. My parents don't believe in caging animals. He has a pet door to the back patio. Sometimes we don't see him for a few hours but he always comes home, especially when it's time to eat. He's a good rabbit, Theo, a member of the family. We've had him for five years. What're they going to do to him, Theo?" His lip quivered and his voice cracked and

Theo was afraid the kid might start bawling right there in the hallway. It was obvious that Rufus's arrest had rocked him and probably his family.

"Well, it depends on what's proven in court. If Rufus is found guilty and considered a public threat or nuisance, Animal Control can keep him." And they can also put the rabbit to sleep forever, but Theo wasn't about to go that far. Roger was obviously fragile and couldn't take such dreadful news.

"He's just a lop-eared rabbit, Theo, not a dangerous animal," Roger said, his voice rising. "None of this makes sense."

"Look, it says that the hearing is today at four o'clock in Animal Court in the courthouse." Theo knew he had little time to prepare. He also knew what Roger was about to ask.

"Will you take the case, Theo? Everyone says you're the best in Animal Court. They say you've never lost a case there."

Theo's chest swelled with pride. The truth was that his record in Animal Court was six wins and no losses, though no one was keeping score but him. He certainly couldn't brag about it because none of his friends would understand. Few of them had ever heard of Animal Court.

It was impossible to say no. His parents believed that a big part of being a lawyer was using your position to help those in need, regardless of their ability to pay. At the age of thirteen, and still without a license, Theo couldn't exactly charge for his services, so he never worried about the fee part. It would be cruel to leave poor Rufus detained by Animal Control while Roger and his family worried themselves sick over their beloved rabbit.

He gritted his teeth, looked Roger squarely in the eyes, put a hand on his shoulder, and said, "Okay, I'll do it. See you there at four o'clock."

Theo entered the courthouse basement room reserved for Animal Court at ten minutes before four p.m., and found a sparse gathering, which was a relief. In the past some of his cases had attracted big crowds and that added pressure. As much as he dreamed of the courtroom, when the trials actually arrived he always preferred smaller crowds. He had a knot in his stomach, as always. He'd once heard an old lawyer say: "If you're not nervous in a courtroom, then you're in the wrong place."

The courtroom was divided in half by a center aisle, with rows of folding chairs on both sides. In the front row, Theo saw Roger and went to greet him. Roger was with his mother, a nervous-looking woman with short blond hair in a weird green T-shirt.

They were relieved to see Theo. Roger said, "This is my mother, Alice Kerr." She squeezed Theo's hand as if she were drowning and said, "Theo, it's a pleasure to meet you. Roger says Rufus is in good hands."

"Thanks. I'll do my best."

"They won't . . ." She placed her hands rather awkwardly over Roger's ears and continued, "Put him to sleep, will they?" Roger squirmed and hissed, "Mom! Come on!"

"It's unlikely," Theo said in a low voice as he tried to ignore the little drama. "I've never seen it happen. The judge has to find that the animal is a persistent and continuing threat to the public and that nothing else can be done."

As he talked, he noticed a young curly-haired woman walking down the aisle with a stack of folders under her arm. She was dressed professionally and had an important air about her. Theo had seen her a couple of times around the courthouse and figured she was the newest hire in the District Attorney's office. Jack Hogan usually sent his rookies all the way down to Animal Court to get their feet wet with easy trial work. She set her stack of paperwork down on the flimsy table used by the prosecution and opened a file as if preparing for major litigation.

Theo nodded and Roger and Alice stepped forward with him to the defense table. The rookie walked over, stuck out her hand, offered a big smile, and said, "I'm Brittany Collins, with the DA's office."

Theo shook her hand and said, "I'm Theodore Boone, for the defense."

She was amused by the size and age of her opponent, but kept smiling. She was very cute and Theo liked her immediately. "And you represent who?" she asked.

"Rufus the rabbit. The first case on the docket."

"Ah, of course. This little guy has caused quite a stir in town." Brittany turned and nodded toward the spectators. An impressive crowd was suddenly gathering in the seats behind the prosecution's table. Whatever Rufus had been doing had evidently ticked off a lot of people. And they were still filing in.

Great, thought Theo. The whole courtroom was against him.

It suddenly hit Theo that he was completely unprepared, a cardinal sin for a trial lawyer. He had not had the time during the day to meet with his client and gather evidence. On top of that, Animal Court did not permit discovery and was often a trial by ambush. Often there were no lawyers at all, just parties representing themselves as they argued over barking dogs and stray cows.

Brittany flashed another cute smile and said, "Take it easy on me today, Theo."

"Uh, what do you mean?"

"I hear you're a killer in Animal Court." She winked and flitted away, and Theo couldn't think of anything to say. He glanced again at the crowd and noticed that most were well-dressed. Animal Court often attracted a lower end crowd, rougher folks who didn't hire lawyers and had more problems with their animals.

Theo swallowed hard and wondered what he'd gotten himself into. Rufus seemed like a run-of-the-mill Animal Court case. He'd tried a half dozen of them, but now he had a case he hadn't prepared for and he was dealing with a cute assistant DA who made him nervous. Theo had learned from his parents not to trust the pleasant chatter of lawyers before the real action, whether in trial or in negotiation. Every lawyer has a job to do, and just because one is chatty beforehand doesn't mean he or she will not pull every trick possible to prevail. Brittany's charm worried Theo. She would no doubt catch the eye of Judge Yeck.

Theo returned to his seat next to Roger and his mother and whispered, "Any idea why all of these people are here? Tell me now so I won't get blindsided."

Alice shook her head. No.

Roger said, "Not really. All we know is that Rufus is always sound asleep when we go to bed, but in the mornings he comes in covered with dirt and briars. I have to bathe him every morning. He goes roaming at night, but we have no idea where."

"Great," Theo mumbled.

An Animal Control officer standing by the bench yelled, "Keep your seats. Animal Court is now in session. The Honorable Sergio Yeck presiding."

Judge Yeck ambled through a side door and took his seat behind the rickety bench. As always, he wore jeans and cowboy boots, no robe whatsoever. He was a local lawyer with a colorful history and the only lawyer in town who had agreed to serve as a part-time judge in Animal Court. He liked to grumble about the job, but his friends knew that he secretly enjoyed it.

"Good afternoon, Ms. Collins," he said with a wide smile.

"Good afternoon, Judge," she replied. It was immediately obvious to Theo that these two had met before. He knew from experience that Judge Yeck had an eye for pretty ladies.

"And always good to see you, Theo," he said.

"Thanks, Judge. Always nice to be here."

His Honor looked at his docket and said, "So our first matter is the detention of Mr. Rufus the Rabbit. Theo, I assume you are representing the Kerr family, the owners of Rufus."

Without standing, Theo nodded and said, "Yes, sir."

"All right, Ms. Collins, you get to go first. Let's hear it and please keep it brief."

Brittany stood rather professionally with a yellow legal pad, though standing was not required. She began, "Well, Your Honor, there are numerous complaining parties. It seems as though every night for the past two weeks the entire neighborhood along Oakleaf and Market Streets comes to life with a loud and prolonged chorus of barking dogs. House dogs, yard dogs, stray dogs, all dogs become extremely agitated and bark and howl for hours, as if on cue. The racket goes on and on and no one is getting any sleep. These people, many of whom are here in the courtroom, are exhausted, and they are fed up."

Theo glanced over his shoulder, a mistake. The courtroom was packed with folks who looked tired and fed up.

"About what time does this show begin each night?" Judge Yeck asked.

"It's really strange, Judge. It starts at precisely midnight, under clear skies or under clouds. At the stroke of midnight the dogs seem to go nuts. A house pet can be sound asleep until he hears a distant bark, then he or she goes crazy. It spreads quickly throughout the neighborhood and all the lights come on. Everybody's awake."

"You have a witness?" Judge Yeck asked, gazing at the packed courtroom.

"I have at least twenty."

"Well, we don't need twenty. I think I already get the message. Pick your best two and let's hear them."

"Okay. The City calls Ms. Emma Dofield."

Ms. Dofield stood and hustled to the front. She was a pleasant-looking lady of about fifty. She stopped in front of the bench, raised her right hand and swore to tell the truth, then took a seat in a folding chair.

Brittany simply said, "Now, Ms. Dofield, please tell us your story."

The witness couldn't wait. "Well, you've already heard what we're going through. It's terrible. We're exhausted. The dogs are all acting weird, and not just at night. We had to take Leo to the dog shrink."

Judge Yeck leaned in and said, "Excuse me, who's Leo?"

"Our dog. He's a Lagotto."

"A what?"

"A Lagotto. An Italian water dog."

"Of course. And he went to the shrink?"

"Yes, sir. He's a bit neurotic to begin with, but a very

sweet little guy. He's been so upset with all this that we had to put him on antidepressants."

"Anyway."

"Anyway, two nights ago I was awake at midnight, sort of waiting for the fireworks, and sure enough things erupted on time. Leo, who's a bit groggy these days but nonetheless still alert, ran to the window in the breakfast nook and started barking at the patio. I eased to a window in the den, and in the shadows I saw a rabbit. A big rabbit. He jumped onto our deck, which is made of wood, and started thumping his back foot real loud. He did this little dance in a circle, thumping like crazy, rattling the boards, and driving Leo even crazier. There were no lights on our patio so I turned on the floodlight, but the rabbit had vanished. I turned it off, waited and waited, and sure enough he came back. I could make out his silhouette in the shadows. He started thumping again, real loud, but when I reached for the light, he vanished again. It was like he has a sixth sense and knows when the lights are about to come on."

Brittany asked, "So, can you describe this rabbit?"

"Well, sort of. He's big, bigger than any rabbit I've ever seen, and he has these really floppy ears."

Brittany turned to Theo and said, "Your witness."

Theo was on his feet, holding his yellow legal pad like

all lawyers. He smiled politely at the witness and said, "Now, Ms. Dofield, you're certain this rabbit is a male."

"Uh, well, uh, to be honest, I don't really know."

"But you have repeatedly referred to the rabbit as 'he' and 'him.' Correct?"

"Sure, but I guess that's just a habit."

"Fair enough. You don't know the gender. Do you know its color?"

"Beg your pardon."

"Ms. Dofield, you said it's very dark on your patio and there's no light. You saw a silhouette in the shadows. Is the rabbit white, gray, brown, black, yellow, spotted? Please describe this rabbit."

"Well, I would say dark."

"Dark gray, dark brown, black?"

"I really don't know for sure."

"Okay. According to the Atlas Register of Animals, there are about ninety different breeds of rabbit. What kind of rabbit are we talking about here?"

"Oh, I have no idea."

"No further questions, Your Honor."

"You may return to your seat," Judge Yeck said with a smile. He wanted to wink at Theo but that would not have been professional. "Call your second witness," he said.

Brittany stood. "The City calls the Honorable Frank Pendergrast."

Theo almost fainted. He felt as though he'd been in Youth Court every day for the past month lobbying Judge Pendergrast on behalf of Woody and Tony. Now he was supposed to cross-examine him?

And how fair was a trial when one of the witnesses was a well-respected judge? Theo wanted to object to his testimony but could think of no good reason. Plus, he knew Judge Yeck was going to allow his colleague to testify anyway.

After he took his oath and had a seat, Brittany wasted no time. "Judge Pendergrast, you are one of three neighbors who signed the complaint. Would you explain why?"

"Sure. Just like Ms. Dofield said, this has been going on for about two weeks. My wife and I have a bloodhound named Barney who sleeps downstairs and he's been very upset. You ever heard a bloodhound howl indoors at midnight?"

"No, sir, don't think so."

"Well, it's something to remember. Last Sunday night I hurried downstairs and I was sitting with Barney, trying to settle him down. I could hear dogs barking for miles around it seemed. I saw something on the patio that I first thought was a big rat. We've had a problem with them. I reached for a light, turned it on, and the thing vanished, just like that. No sign at all. I turned the light off, waited, and then I heard this thumping sound on the patio. Barney went nuts again. I eased to the window and caught a glimpse of the varmint. It wasn't a rat, it was a rabbit, a huge rabbit with brown fur and big hind legs. He was thumping away, turning in a circle like some kind of war dance. I reached for the light again, flipped the switch, but he was gone."

"Then what happened?"

"I turned the light off and waited, but he had moved on. Barney was agitated for the rest of the night and I could hear dogs barking throughout the neighborhood."

"What did you do then?"

"Well, as you might guess, these escapades have caused quite a stir in our neighborhood. Fred Koger lives four doors down and he knows the Kerrs, who live about three blocks away. He had seen their rabbit, this Rufus character, and he knew that the Kerrs allowed him to run free at night. They supposedly have a pet door and don't believe in caging their animals. We put our heads together and decided to notify Animal Control. Here we are."

Brittany said, "Your Honor, at this time I'd like to bring in the defendant."

Judge Yeck said, "Sure, bring him in."

An Animal Control officer opened a door, disappeared, then came back with a large cage which he set on a table under the bench. Everyone stretched their necks to get a look at the criminal. Rufus chewed on some kale leaves, seemingly unconcerned.

Brittany pointed at him and asked, "Now, Judge Pendergrast, is this the rabbit you saw on your patio two nights ago?"

"I believe so, yes."

"Thank you. I tender the witness," Brittany said and took her seat.

Theo rose slowly, horrified that he was expected to cross-examine a judge he had great respect for. Plus, he was a nervous wreck because the courtroom was now packed. Even more, he was just a thirteen-year-old kid fighting a bunch of adults.

He smiled at the witness, and Judge Pendergrast smiled back because it was, after all, sort of cute to be facing a kid lawyer.

Theo swallowed hard and plowed ahead. "Judge Pendergrast, according to your testimony, your patio is dark at night, correct?"

"That's right."

"And in order to have lights you have to flip a switch from the inside?"

"Yes."

"So it was around midnight, it was dark, and you saw something on your patio?"

"That's what I said, Theo."

"Would you please look at Rufus? Would you agree that his fur is light brown with a few white spots, and that he is quite large for a rabbit?"

"I suppose so."

"And would you agree that he looks nothing like a rat?"

"No, he doesn't, but that was just my first impression. I got a better look a few minutes later."

"In the dark?"

"Well, yes it was dark."

"In fact, you never saw the rabbit with the lights on?"

"I did not."

"And for the past two weeks you've been exhausted and not sleeping much. Could that affect your eyesight?"

"Maybe, but it didn't. I saw that rabbit, Theo. I'm sure of it."

"Okay. Judge, do you know how many other rabbits are kept as pets in your neighborhood?"

Judge Pendergrast sighed as if frustrated with the entire

episode. And it was a bit demeaning for such an important judge to be sitting down in the basement in Animal Court and getting roughed up by a thirteen-year-old.

"No, I don't know. Do you?"

"I'm asking the questions, Your Honor. Is Rufus the only rabbit in the neighborhood?"

"I do not know."

"Thank you, sir. I have no more questions."

Brittany jumped to her feet and said, "I have just one more, Your Honor."

"Go ahead." Judge Yeck was already bored with the case.

Brittany said, "Now, Judge, you and the others signed the complaint Monday morning, and Rufus was taken into custody, right?"

"That's correct."

"Any noise last night?"

"Not a peep. Everyone slept well for the first time in two weeks."

"The City rests its case, Your Honor." She sat down and Judge Pendergrast returned to his seat in the rear of the crowd.

Judge Yeck looked at Theo and said, "For the defense?"

Theo said, "Well, yes, Your Honor, the defense calls Ms. Alice Kerr."

She swore to tell the truth and took the stand. Before she said anything she looked at the cage as if she might cry.

Theo plowed ahead. "Now, Ms. Kerr, are you the owner of this rabbit?"

"Well, uh, yes I guess. He's owned by our family."

"Tell us a little about Rufus." Theo thought it might be important to learn a little about the animal before Judge Yeck decided whether or not to put it down.

She offered a goofy smile and said, "Oh, he's just marvelous. Rufus is a French Lop, lop-eared, of course, as you can see, and he's quite large for the breed. Most weigh between ten and fifteen pounds, but Rufus is pushing twenty. Eats all the time. We bought him one Easter maybe five years ago and the kids have sort of grown up with Rufus. He's a member of our family."

"And where does he stay in the house?"

"All over the place. He has a small bed in the washroom next to the dryer, and that's where the kids feed him, but he roams as he pleases."

"Can he leave the house whenever he wants?"

"I suppose. We have a small pet gate in the kitchen door so he can go into the backyard if he wants. He does it all the time, especially in warm weather."

"Is the backyard fenced in?"

"It is, of course. Rufus is always confined. I've never known him to roam the neighborhood like these people are saying."

"Can he jump over the fence?"

"Oh, I don't think so. I've never seen him do that. He's very well behaved."

"During the past two weeks, have you noticed anything unusual about Rufus?"

"Well, yes, to be truthful, we've . . ."

"Please be truthful, Ms. Kerr," Judge Yeck said. "You are under oath, remember?"

"Yes, sir. We've noticed that first thing in the mornings Rufus has been covered with dirt, mud, and briars. We checked the back fence and found no way for him to escape, but I just don't know. We've had to bathe him every morning."

Suddenly, Rufus came to life and began pounding the floor of his cage with a hind leg. The cage shook and rattled loudly and began rocking itself toward the edge of the table. Rufus appeared frantic and distraught and began pawing at the cage door with his front feet. He wheezed and sort of shrieked as if he wanted to bark or howl but wasn't sure how to go about it.

Ms. Kerr was alarmed and exclaimed, "Poor thing. He's

so upset. He's never been in a cage before. See what they've done to him."

Rufus turned his rear to the courtroom, froze for a second, and passed gas, not loudly, but in a potent concentration. The odor was instant and strong and when he was finished he began pounding the bottom of the cage again.

Judge Yeck snarled at the Animal Control officer, "Take him away." The poor guy approached the cage timidly, lifted it, and rushed Rufus away from the bench, through the door, and out of sight.

The odor lingered for a moment. Judge Yeck had had enough. "You finished, Theo?"

It was more of a command than a question and Theo said, "Yes, sir."

"Cross-examination, Ms. Collins?"

Brittany stood and wisely said, "Judge, I think we've had enough. I'd like to propose a settlement here to avoid the sticky issue of putting down Rufus. The City really doesn't want to do that, not at this time anyway."

"Oh, thank goodness!" Ms. Kerr said from the witness chair and covered her mouth with both hands.

Judge Yeck said, "Ms. Kerr, you may return to your seat. Let me see the lawyers up here, please."

Theo strutted to the bench as if he'd been trying cases

for twenty years. Brittany smiled at him and said, "After you." They stepped to the bench and Judge Yeck leaned down low. In a whisper he said, "I'm going to spare his life, this time, but next time I'll order a firing squad." He smiled at his humor. The lawyers did not. He waved the air in front of his face as the last of the odor slowly evaporated.

Yeck continued. "There must be a simple way to keep this rabbit in the house at night, right, Theo? Can't they just lock the pet door?"

"I don't see why not, Your Honor."

"Sounds simple to me," Brittany said.

Judge Yeck looked at the crowd and said, "Okay, this matter is resolved. I am ordering Rufus the Rabbit to be returned to his owner immediately. And he will be on probation. I am ordering the Kerr family to keep this rabbit indoors during the night, every night, and if he gets out again and torments the neighbors' dogs, then I will have no choice but to order his arrest and extermination. Do you understand, Ms. Kerr?"

She was still crying, but she wiped her cheeks and nodded. Yes.

"Any questions, Theo?"

"No, sir. And thanks, Your Honor."

The crowd hurried out. Most of the neighbors seemed

relieved that the defendant would now be kept under lock and key. Rufus was handed over to Roger and Ms. Kerr, who cuddled him like a newborn.

Outside the courthouse, they thanked Theo and congratulated him over and over.

As he rode away on his bike, he couldn't help but whisper proudly: "Seven wins, no losses."

CHAPTER 17

Garth Tucker's family owned a construction company that built cheap motels along interstate highways. Garth's father inherited the company from his father and had the reputation of being a shrewd businessman. It therefore came as no surprise when he hired Clifford Nance to defend his son.

Clifford Nance was perhaps the finest criminal defense lawyer for miles around. Theo had watched him in court many times, most recently in the murder trial of Pete Duffy. When Clifford Nance was in trial, the charges were serious and the accused had plenty of money to hire the best.

At nine a.m. on a Wednesday morning, Nance sat at the defense table with young Garth next to him. For the occasion, Garth wore a dark suit and a tie, and he had evidently just been to the barbershop. He was a handsome young gentleman who looked as though he was not capable of committing any crime. His father sat behind him.

Judge Gantry was on the bench, shuffling papers and working his way through a crowded docket. He said, "Good morning. The first matter of business is the preliminary hearing for Mr. Garth Tucker. Let the record reflect that the accused is present along with his attorney, Mr. Clifford Nance. Is the State ready to proceed?"

Jack Hogan, the veteran prosecutor, stood and said, "Yes, Your Honor. I believe you have the police report and the summary of the charges."

"I do. And I'd like to remind everyone that this is only a preliminary hearing, not a trial, so let's be brief."

"Indeed. The State calls Mr. Clem Hamm to the stand."

Mr. Hamm was waiting by the jury box and stepped forward to be sworn. Once situated in the witness chair, he smiled at His Honor and tried not to appear nervous. Jack Hogan asked some basic questions to establish that he was a part owner of Kall's Grocery, an all-night convenience store on Highway 22 north of town. On the evening of October 18, around eleven p.m., he was behind the counter going about his business, which was slow that night. No one else was in the store. A young man walked in, went to the beer cooler, grabbed a case of beer, brought it to the counter, said he was out of money, reached into a pocket and whipped out a pistol. He aimed it squarely at Clem's face and told him to open the cash register, which he did. Clem took a step back, held up his hands, and said please don't shoot.

"Do you see the man with the gun in this courtroom?" Hogan asked.

"Right there," Clem said, pointing at Garth.

"What happened next?"

"He grabbed the cash, stuffed it in a pocket, picked up the beer, and as he was leaving he pointed the gun at my nose and pulled the trigger. I almost fainted. Warm water hit me in the eyes. He laughed and said, "*Bang, bang*. Don't call the cops or I'll blast you again."

"And what did you do then?"

"Well, for a second or two, I was too scared to move, so I just stood there. Then I heard his car door slam, so I stepped to the window and watched him drive away, spinning tires and slinging gravel. Once he was gone, I ran over, locked the front door, and called the police."

"What kind of car was he driving?"

"A green Mustang, one of those souped-up muscle cars."

"How much money did he take from the cash register?"

"Two hundred and fourteen dollars."

"Now, Mr. Hamm, when he aimed the pistol at you, did you realize it was only a toy?"

"No, sir, not at all. The thing looked real and I was scared to death. I thought I was a dead man. I mean, my heart froze and I couldn't breathe for a moment or two."

Hogan stepped to a table below the bench and picked up a pistol in a plastic bag. He slowly removed it and handed it to Clem. "This look familiar?"

Clem took it, examined it, and said, "This looks just like the one he aimed at me."

"Thank you." Hogan took the pistol and placed it back on the table. "Now, Mr. Hamm, does your store use surveillance cameras?"

"Yes, sir, got 'em all over the place."

The lights were dimmed as Jack Hogan rolled over a large screen. Four of the cameras recorded Garth's quick visit to Kall's. The first camera was outside and looked down at the gas pumps. In one corner it showed the Mustang arrive and Garth hopping out. Seconds later it showed him returning to his car with the case of beer. The second camera was mounted inside and caught customers coming and going. There was Garth, crystal clear, as he entered the store and looked around. Not long afterward it recorded him leaving with the beer. The third camera was mounted high in the rear of the store and faced the large coolers filled with beer, bottled water, and soft drinks. Garth yanked open a door, grabbed the beer, and disappeared. The fourth camera was hidden above the cash register and, in vivid detail, showed him put the beer on the counter, pull out the pistol, say something to Clem, grab the cash, then aim and pull the trigger.

What kind of idiot robs a store with such heavy surveillance?

In the front row of the courtroom, Woody and Tony sat next to their lawyer, Rodney Wall. They would not participate in the preliminary hearing, but Mr. Wall wanted them there anyway. It was important to see the evidence the State had at its disposal. As Clem described each video, Rodney Wall leaned over to Tony and whispered, "This guy is a moron."

Tony nodded his agreement and whispered, "He claims he was drunk and didn't know what he was doing."

Mr. Wall just shook his head. None of the videos revealed any trace of the Lambert boys in the car.

The lights were turned on and Clem Hamm stepped down. The next witness was a detective in a dark suit. Jack Hogan handed him the pistol and asked him to identify it. He said, "We found this in the left front pocket of Mr. Garth Tucker. It's a plastic water pistol that is designed to look exactly like a compact Ruger nine millimeter. And, I must say, it is a very good fake. The detail is impressive. From a distance of ten feet, I could not tell the difference between this and the real thing."

"Who makes these?"

"I don't know where it came from, but we found a toy company in Taiwan that makes water guns of all varieties. Evidently, there are several manufacturers."

Woody agreed. He still remembered the horror of staring at the pistol as Garth pulled the trigger. For that split second, he was too stunned to realize what was happening.

"Nothing further, Your Honor," Jack Hogan said. "The State requests that this case be sent to the grand jury for further action."

Judge Gantry said, "Mr. Nance?"

Clifford Nance half-stood and said, "Nothing at this time, Your Honor." It was neither the time nor the place to argue on behalf of his client. Like most good criminal defense lawyers, Mr. Nance was using the occasion to see the evidence and to measure the witnesses to be used against Garth.

And he had seen enough. The case would never go to trial, never get near a jury. Nance was already working on a scheme to keep Garth out of jail, and it involved the two juveniles who had been riding with him.

CHAPTER 18

At four p.m. on Friday afternoon, Major Ludwig gave the command and thirty-nine Boy Scouts hopped aboard the troop's old green school bus and set off for Lake Marlo, two hours away. Their tents and gear were packed neatly in the rear of the bus. Up front, the Major relaxed with three older guys who made up the Old Goats Patrol. The three were fathers of Scouts and had been invited for the weekend.

Theo's dad had accompanied the troop on two occasions, but he was not much of an outdoors type. Theo, though, lived for the monthly camping trips. As the leader of the Falcon Patrol, he had seven Scouts under his command, and he was in charge of planning the meals, organizing work details, and setting up camp. The Major handled any disciplinary problems, of which there were few. The boys were excellent Scouts and the Major, a retired Marine pilot, pushed them hard to improve their outdoors skills and knowledge. They genuinely respected him and never wanted to disappoint.

Theo was sitting next to Woody, the assistant patrol leader. A week earlier he had been sitting in jail as Theo and his friends scrambled desperately to get him out. Once freed, he was reluctant to go camping. The cost was about fifty dollars per Scout, for food and supplies, and Woody was not about to ask his mother for the money. Theo and the others knew better than to mention a loan because Woody was too proud. At the last minute, Tony stepped up with the money and insisted that his little brother take the trip. The Major was also involved. He called Daisy Lambert and urged her to encourage Woody to go.

Neither Tony nor Woody had missed school since their release. Both seemed to have found a new enthusiasm for class and homework. Though they worried about their legal problems, they believed in their innocence and were confident things would work out. Woody certainly seemed happier and was excited about the campout.

Lake Marlo was the troop's favorite destination. It was a large man-made lake inside a state park with dozens of campsites and trails and streams for fishing. No development had been allowed, so there were no beach houses or condos or cabins cluttering the landscape. The lake was an endless wilderness, the perfect place for a Scout troop to retreat to for a long weekend away from civilization. The bus entered the park at dusk and the road went from asphalt to gravel. The Major preferred the remote camping areas, away from the nicer campsites with indoor plumbing and RV hookups. As the road turned to dirt, the bus seemed to disappear into a dense jungle. When the road finally stopped, on a small rise at the edge of the lake, the Scouts hustled off the bus and unloaded their gear.

The Major huddled with the patrol leaders and they agreed on the layout. Each patrol would pitch tents around a common area where a fire pit would be established. Darkness was approaching and there wasn't much time to cook, which was typical on Friday nights. Dinner was usually sandwiches and chips, with more elaborate meals planned for the weekend. Most of the Scouts were working on their Cooking merit badge and its requirements called for such delicacies as homemade biscuits and bread, pot roast, omelets, and grilled fish, assuming they were caught from nearby streams.

Theo had already added Cooking to his sash, along with twenty-four other merit badges. If things went as planned, he would achieve the coveted rank of Eagle in about a year.

His father and the Major were encouraging him to speed up because his life would change dramatically after the eighth grade. When he entered high school, there would be distractions.

Once the tents were pitched in a neat half circle around the fire pit, the Scouts cut wood, dug a latrine, lashed together tables, secured the food, and finally ate dinner. They were excited and there was all manner of joking, laughter, horseplay, and friendly trash-talking. With no other campers within miles, the Major was content to let the boys have their fun.

After cleanup, when the sky was dark, they gathered by patrol and listened to their instructions. The "Midnight Hike" was one of their favorites and the Major laid down the rules. He would lead with the Falcon Patrol behind him, then, a few yards back, Ranger, Warthog, Rattlesnake, and Panther. The Old Goats Patrol would bring up the rear and hopefully collect any Scouts who fell behind. The trails were narrow and the hikers would move slowly in single file. Each patrol leader would use a flashlight. They would climb steadily to a ridge with a view of the lake, at least an hour away, then retreat back down the trail.

For added drama, the Major cautioned them to look out for snakes, bears, even coyotes. This only added to their excitement. Like a real soldier, he growled "Forward March," and away they went. Thirty-nine Scouts and four adults.

It was almost ten when they returned to the campsite, exhausted. Wood was added to the fire pit and the troop gathered around it. The temperature had dropped considerably and the night had turned chilly.

The principal job of the Old Goats Patrol, other than a little supervision and bonding with the kids, was to tell ghost stories around the campfire. The Major encouraged the dads to work on their stories and perfect frightening tales that would terrify the boys and have them jumping out of their skins. A few months earlier, Justin's father had told the story of a legendary coyote that stalked campers in the area, and Mr. Closkey somehow rigged up a hidden boom box that erupted in the bloodcurdling scream of a deranged wolf. With perfect timing the animal roared in the darkness. The Scouts shrieked in terror and grabbed one another. When the mad dog finally stopped, the boys managed to relax a little when they realized the geezers were on the ground laughing. The Major could not have been prouder.

The first story was about the ghost of a man who had drowned in the lake. For years campers had reported seeing an eerie light out on the water in the middle of the night. Then one night it began moving toward the shore and a voice could be heard. A family of four was camping near the water, and they watched in horror as the light grew brighter and brighter. Their bodies were found a week later, floating on the water, far away from their campsite.

It was a nice story, frightening enough, and it held the boys' attention. The second story was about a mysterious creature that was eerily similar to Bigfoot. His legend was that for decades he had roamed around Lake Marlo stealing food from campers and in general terrorizing the place.

After three ghost tales, the boys were sufficiently spooked and the Major ordered lights out. They hustled to their tents, zipped up the doors tight, turned off their flashlights, and nestled snugly into their sleeping bags. As the night became quiet, they waited nervously for ghosts and savage animals to attack. The Major walked around quietly, smiling at the sounds of the whispered conversations as they trailed off and his tired men fell asleep.

The night passed without incident. At sunrise, the Major and the dads staggered from their tents, stretched and shook off the stiffness of a night on the ground, and began making coffee as loudly as possible. Slowly, the Scouts appeared, most of them still in the uniforms they'd slept in. Cooking fires were built and breakfast was soon under way.

The Major asked Woody to help him gather firewood, and they hiked to a secluded area not far from the campsite. The Major pointed to a spot on a boulder and they sat down. He said, "Look, Woody, I'm not sure you know it, but I do a lot of volunteer work in Youth Court, and I'm aware of your case. Do you mind talking about it?"

"No, sir, I guess not," Woody replied.

"Often Judge Pendergrast will ask me to review a case and try to help the family. I have not looked at your file but I understand there are some serious charges. You want to tell me about it?"

"Sure." The truth was that Woody, like every other Scout, would trust the Major with anything. So Woody told the story of the "armed robbery." And the beer drinking. The Major listened thoughtfully without passing judgment.

When Woody finished, the Major said, "Sounds like you were hanging out with the wrong crowd."

"It wasn't a crowd, and my brother Tony did nothing wrong. We had no idea what Garth was up to. It's just so unfair."

"It sounds unfair. And Tony will tell the same story?"

"It's not a story, Major, it's the truth."

"Okay. What is Garth's version?"

"I'm not sure. I haven't talked to him lately, but the night we were arrested he told the police that the water pistol was mine. A total lie. He thinks that if I go along with his lie, then we'll all get off light because I'm only thirteen. Plus, he's got a big-time lawyer now so who knows what they'll say."

"And your lawyer is Rodney Wall?"

"Yes, sir. I'm not sure he believes us. I wish we could get another lawyer but we can't afford one."

"I know Rodney Wall. We've worked a couple of cases together."

"Is he a good lawyer?"

"He's new on the job, been there only about a year. Got a lot to learn but he'll be okay. I can talk to him. Would you like for me to ask the judge if I can help with your case?"

"Sure, Major. That would be great."

"Judge Pendergrast is a good man who has a knack for finding the truth. Things will work out, Woody."

"Thanks. I need some help. Me and Tony."

"Now, about this drinking. I don't like it one bit. You're much too young and it will only lead to more trouble."

"It's no big deal, really. Sometimes Tony and I will sneak a beer out of the fridge, but we really don't have the money for it."

"Are you smoking pot?"

"No, sir."

"Is Tony?"

"Probably, but never around me."

"Your parents are divorced?"

"Yes, sir. My dad lives in the county but we don't see much of him. My mom is remarried to a guy who's okay, but he does construction out of town and we don't see much of him. She works two jobs, sometimes three."

"So there's not much supervision at home."

"No, sir."

The Major slowly got to his feet and paced around, deep in thought. He said, "Let's deal with the drinking first. It's against the law and I want it stopped. Okay?"

"Yes, sir. No problem. I don't even like the taste of it."

"Beer and alcohol can only lead to trouble, especially for a teenager. You're promising me right now that it won't happen again?"

"Yes, sir."

"Good. I'll make sure the judge understands this. And no more missing school, okay?"

"Okay."

"No drinking, no skipping, and hit the books hard. I'll check with your teachers and monitor your progress. Judge Pendergrast will want to know how you're doing. If I'm on the case, Woody, I expect a lot of improvement. You're too young and too smart to fall through the cracks. Understood?"

"Yes, sir."

"I'll speak to your mother. Mind if I have a little chat with Tony? I suspect he's not a positive influence these days."

"He's a good guy, Major. We've seen the inside of the jail and we don't want to go back there."

"Good. Maybe this little brush with the law will be a good thing."

"You ever been arrested, Major?"

"No."

"It's no fun. I can still feel the handcuffs clamping on my wrists. I can still see the cops frowning at me, still see their angry faces, still smell the nasty jail. The whole thing was scary because you have no control over anything and you don't know what will happen next." Woody bit his lip as his eyes watered and he began shaking.

The Major walked over and put a hand on his shoulder. "It's going to be okay, Woody."

CHAPTER 19

The troop returned to civilization late Sunday afternoon. As the bus entered Strattenburg, the boys were silent. They were exhausted but also in a somber mood. The returns were always like that. The planning, the anticipation, the sheer fun of being in the woods for the weekend—it all came crashing down as they reentered the real world and life returned to normal. Tomorrow meant school! It was hard to believe. It seemed cruel.

Of Mr. Mount's sixteen boys in homeroom, seven were Scouts who had gone camping. As soon as the bell rang Monday morning and he took roll—all sixteen were present—he asked Woody to stand before the class and describe the weekend. Being thirteen years old, most of the boys preferred not to speak before a group, though Theo loved to do so. To overcome this shyness, Mr. Mount often selected one at random and asked him to walk to the front of the room and talk. He expected them to have good posture, speak slowly, and be as confident as possible. A few were naturals but most struggled for five long minutes.

Woody began by telling a funny story about a prank they played on the youngest Scout. He got a few laughs, seemed to warm up, and as he was describing the Midnight Hike there was a knock on the door. Mrs. Gladwell interrupted things as she walked in. She nodded at Mr. Mount, then at Woody, and asked them to step into the hall.

Mr. Bob Hawley from Action Bail Bonds was waiting. He introduced himself to Mr. Mount and asked Woody, "Did you leave town last weekend?"

Woody glanced nervously at Mrs. Gladwell and said, "Yes, sir. I went camping with the Scouts to Lake Marlo."

"That's what I heard," Mr. Hawley growled. "You're not supposed to leave Stratten County, son. You violated the terms of your bail bond." He whipped out a pair of handcuffs and grabbed Woody's arm. "You're coming with me."

Mr. Mount took a step forward and said, "You can't do that!"

"Sure I can, do it all the time when the criminals skip bail."

"Don't call him a criminal!" Mrs. Gladwell said.

Woody jerked his arm away, but Hawley managed to grab the other arm tightly and slap the cuffs on his right wrist. "Let him go!" Mr. Mount said.

The door was partially open and Theo and the others heard every word.

Hawley was a tough guy who knew his business. "You got no choice, kid, and don't start trouble." He poked Mr. Mount in the chest and said, "And if you get in the way I have the authority to arrest you as well. Now back off."

He grabbed Woody's left wrist and cuffed it. "Let's go."

"Where are we going?" Woody asked loudly.

"To jail, son. That's where we take all the bail jumpers."

"He didn't jump bail," Mr. Mount said, though he wasn't sure.

"Knock it off," Hawley said angrily and seemed ready to throw a punch. Mrs. Gladwell backed away, speechless. Hawley grabbed Woody by the elbow and marched him down the hall. Fortunately, it was empty. The students were still in homeroom and waiting for the bell for first period.

The remaining fifteen boys raced to the windows and watched in disbelief as Woody was led out of the building. Another tough-looking guy was waiting beside a car and opened a rear door. Hawley shoved Woody into the back seat.

Mr. Mount looked dazed when he reentered the classroom. The boys scrambled back to their seats. For a moment, nothing was said. The unbelievable moment spoke for itself. Finally Mr. Mount said, "Theo, did you know Woody was not supposed to leave the county?"

"Of course not. It never crossed my mind, or his, or anyone else's for that matter. I can't believe this."

"I can't either."

"How can they do that?" Aaron asked. "That guy's not a cop is he?"

"No, he's not," Mr. Mount said, rubbing his jaw. "But a bail bondsman does have the authority to arrest his own client if the terms of the bond are violated."

Mrs. Gladwell stepped through the door and said, "Mr. Mount, would you and Theo come to my office?"

As if on cue, the bell for first period rang and the boys slowly picked up their backpacks. Theo and Mr. Mount followed Mrs. Gladwell to her office where she closed the door. She stood beside her desk and looked at them. None of the three knew what to say.

After a pause she said, "Okay, what do we do now? I assume that guy has the right to go virtually anywhere to grab one of his clients, but it does seem as though a school should be off-limits."

"It's not," Mr. Mount said. "The law gives bail bondsmen a lot of power. But the whole idea of Woody jumping bail is just plain stupid. So he left town. He wasn't trying to run away or skip out. He left, he came back, he showed up here today for school just like he was supposed to. That guy probably hopes the judge will set a new bail so he can write another bond, make another buck off Woody."

"Woody doesn't have another buck," Theo said. "We had to beg and borrow the first time. He'll be stuck in jail forever."

"What should we do?" she asked.

Mr. Mount said, "Well, the first thing is to notify his lawyer, Mr. Wall. They'll take Woody before the judge real soon, I suppose, and his lawyer needs to be there."

"We should be there, too," Theo said, always eager to go to court and avoid class.

"All right," she said. "I'll call his mother. Mr. Mount, you call his lawyer."

Theo suddenly had an idea. He said, "And I'll call Major Ludwig, our scoutmaster. He and Woody talked about his case during the campout, and the Major has volunteered to act as his Youth Court counselor. He knows the judge pretty well."

"Great idea," she said. "Let's get busy."

Woody was placed in the same cell he and Tony had once shared with their old pal Jock, and the memories were cold and harsh. He was in a state of disbelief and mumbled to himself as he stretched out on the bottom bunk and tried to make sense of it all. Alone again, he turned to face the wall and fought back tears. For a solid week, he had not only gone to school every day but had done so with all homework completed. He had stayed after school for tutoring. The thought of a beer had never crossed his mind. He had gone camping with his Scout troop. What else could he have done to behave himself? Yet here he was again, in a dingy jail cell all alone.

An hour later, a jailer walked to his cell and informed him that he would be taken before the judge for a one p.m. hearing. He thanked the man, though he had no idea what was about to happen. He managed to convince himself that his mother and Tony and Theo were doing everything possible to get him out again. He was worried sick, though. If the judge imposed bail again, there was no way they could raise any more money. He would probably get stuck in jail for months.

Lunch was a turkey sandwich and a dill pickle, and he ate every bit because he was starving. The same deputy unlocked his cell, handcuffed him, and led him to the front, past the desk, and to a waiting patrol car. A few minutes later, he entered the basement of the courthouse and rode up the service elevator.

Judge Pendergrast was on the bench when Woody was brought in. In the front row were his mother, Theo, and Mr. Mount. His lawyer, Rodney Wall, was waiting by the bench with Bob Hawley, a man he now despised.

For Theo, it was the first time he'd seen the judge since he cross-examined him in Animal Court. He, Theo, assumed there were no hard feelings. He thought he'd done a good job on cross. He thought the judge had handled himself well as a witness. His Honor was certainly a veteran of courtroom warfare and knew that each lawyer had a job to do. When he assumed the bench he had nodded to Theo but didn't smile. Theo did note that he looked more rested lately. There had been no reports of Rufus rampaging through the neighborhood, no complaints to Animal Control. Theo had bumped into Roger at school and everything was fine with their rabbit.

A fair outcome for all. Who could complain? Theo decided not to worry about any grudge that the judge might carry.

His Honor was reading some paperwork, and when he finished he said, "I've looked over the bond written by Action. Did you, Mr. Lambert, leave the county over the weekend?"

Woody stiffened his back, glared at the judge, and said, "Yes, sir. I went camping at Lake Marlo with my Scout troop."

"And were you aware that you are forbidden from leaving Stratten County?"

"No, sir. I did not know that."

"Mr. Wall, did you warn your client about leaving the county?"

"No, sir. I assumed he and his mother knew that he was expected to stay home."

"Well, it looks as though you assumed too much." Judge Pendergrast seemed irritated at the situation.

The door opened and Major Ludwig walked in. He leaned against the rear wall and nodded at the judge, who noticed him but continued. "Well, I have no choice but to revoke your bond and discuss setting bail."

The Major stepped forward and said, "Your Honor, may it please the court, I have something to say."

"Go ahead, Major Ludwig."

"Woody is one of my Scouts and I'm volunteering as his Youth Court counselor. I take full responsibility for the camping trip and for his leaving the county. It never crossed my mind that he was violating the terms of his bail. It's my fault, Judge, and I can promise you that he will be right here any time you want."

The Major moved and spoke like a seasoned lawyer, and it was obvious he had the judge's respect. He continued. "There is absolutely nothing to be gained by setting bail again. It's my understanding that the family sacrificed everything to get him out the first time. Release him to my supervision and there will be no more problems. I've discussed these charges with Woody, did so last weekend during the campout, and I firmly believe that he is innocent of any serious crime. He has promised me that he will tighten up his study habits, attend school every day, and stay away from the wrong crowd. I'm asking the court to trust me with this matter."

His words were solemn, and when he said "trust" everyone in the courtroom believed him.

Judge Pendergrast scribbled some notes as he pondered the situation. He looked at Woody and said, "Okay, young man, I believe in second chances. I believe this was an honest oversight on your part. I want you and Major Ludwig to report to me at four o'clock every Monday afternoon and we'll discuss your class attendance and your grades. In the meantime, your attorney will get to work on the charges filed against you. You are released on personal identification, no bail."

Woody looked him squarely in the eye and said, "Thank you, Your Honor."

CHAPTER 20

For the next two weeks, Woody managed to avoid another arrest. He didn't miss a day of school, often arrived early and stayed late for extra study hall and tutoring. Tony, too, was back in school and putting more effort into his classwork.

Jail was a place they preferred to avoid.

Clifford Nance had the finest law office in Strattenburg. It occupied the top floors of an old building that was once the only bank in town, and from his large windows he looked down on the courthouse directly across the street. The Yancey River could be seen in the distance. Mr. Nance had bought the building years earlier and spent a lot of money renovating it. His firm had seven lawyers, it was the biggest in town. An elevator ran from the lobby straight to Mr. Nance's suite.

Rodney Wall had never been near the office, though, like most lawyers in town, he had heard descriptions of it. As a young, lowly paid assistant public defender, he dreamed of one day achieving the success of a big-time lawyer like Clifford Nance. He wanted a fancy office, big firm, fine home, foreign cars, the works. And he secretly dreamed of working for the Nance firm. His plan was to gut it out in the trenches of public defender warfare, gain some experience, perhaps start building a reputation, and then apply for an associate's position with the firm. But then a lot of young lawyers in Strattenburg had the same dream.

At the appointed hour, the hour suggested by Mr. Nance, Rodney rode the elevator to the top floor and was greeted by a pretty secretary who offered him coffee. Mr. Nance was on the phone and would be tied up for a moment. Rodney eased into a thick leather chair and admired the Persian rugs and modern art on the walls. He sipped his coffee and stared at his phone, as if he had matters that were far more important than the Lambert case. The secretary typed away. The phones rang occasionally. Finally, a large door opened and Mr. Nance himself stepped out. He waved Rodney into his massive office and pointed to a plush sofa. "Let's sit over here," he said, "and keep things casual."

"Sure," Rodney said as he glanced around. Nance's monument of a work desk was long and wide and appeared to be mahogany, though Rodney wasn't sure. A few files were stacked neatly but for the most part the desk was bare, as if the great man lived an uncluttered life and was concentrating only on the case before him. A conference table with chairs occupied one corner. The walls were covered with paintings and portraits. Everything was neat and perfectly organized, which came as no surprise. Mr. Nance's reputation was that of a trial lawyer who was always thoroughly prepared and organized.

"Nice place you got here," Rodney said as he sank into the sofa.

"Oh, it'll do," Mr. Nance said. He wore a navy suit, crisp white shirt, perfectly knotted tie, expensive shoes, gold watch. Rodney thought to himself: *He probably spends more on clothes in one year than I earn in salary.*

Mr. Nance said, "You know, Rodney, I started in the PD's office thirty years ago. Back then we were in court every day, trying cases. The experience was incredible. How long you been there?"

"A year."

"Monk's a good man. You'll learn a lot from him."

"So far so good."

Enough of the small talk. Mr. Nance cleared his throat as if it were time to move on. He was quite busy. "So, let's talk about this case. The facts are straightforward. Three stupid kids riding around, drinking beer, nothing good was going to happen, right? But nobody got hurt. I mean, you know, it was only a water pistol, a toy. Garth, my client, still maintains that it belonged to the youngest boy—"

"Woody. Woody Lambert. Age thirteen."

"Right. Woody and Tony, but I'm not sure that's true."

"It's not," Rodney said, exerting himself. "It's not true at all. Neither Tony nor Woody had ever seen the pistol before."

"Well, that's what they say, and they are brothers, aren't they?"

"They are, but they seem to be telling the truth."

"No doubt. Look, Rodney, if we fight among ourselves, we all get hurt. I have a plan to get this case dismissed before the grand jury hands down an indictment against my client. Your clients, of course, are not facing indictment because they are minors. I believe I can convince Jack Hogan to cut us a deal and avoid serious charges for these boys. Of course, I'm deeply concerned about my client, Garth, because he is eighteen years old and is being treated like an adult. He's not a bad kid, I assure you of that. Maybe a little immature, but he can outgrow that if he gets the right help. His parents are worried about his drinking and drugs, and he has agreed to submit himself to a treatment facility. This will be very important to Jack Hogan and Judge Gantry. The Tuckers are good people. Garth still plans to go to college. Can you imagine how a felony conviction will haunt him forever? No college. No job. No future."

"How do you avoid a felony?" Rodney asked.

"Start with the gun. I don't need to remind you how much Judge Gantry hates guns and violence. If we allow Woody, the thirteen-year-old, to claim ownership, then the gun loses some of its damage in circuit court. Sure Garth used it for the robbery. Sure that was a really dumb thing to do. But I'll argue that he was not only drinking but already drunk, and thus wasn't sure what he was doing. Woody produced the gun. All three boys were in on the robbery, all three need to be punished. But it's imperative that we avoid a felony, here, Rodney. Are you with me?"

"I get that, but how do you convince Jack Hogan to reduce the armed robbery?"

"By begging. I'll make a strong case that Garth is a good kid who was drunk, and that he was also misguided into believing you can't pull a real robbery with a water pistol, and that nobody got hurt, and that he's real sorry for his mistake, and he'll agree to a few days in jail, two years of probation, a big fine, full restitution to the store, and a hundred hours of volunteer service. Anything to avoid the felony."

"And what about my clients?"

"Come on, Rodney, they're juveniles. Different laws down there in that court. Your boys will get off with a slap on the wrist, a little probation, but nothing serious. Plus they will not have a criminal record."

"But they're innocent, Mr. Nance."

"Just call me Clifford. And they're not completely innocent. They were riding around drinking beer and looking for trouble and they found it. As I understand things, the Lambert boys come from a rough home and they're having trouble at school. This true?"

"That's fair to say."

"Okay, so we take all three boys and we spread around the blame a little. Woody says he owned the gun. He and his brother say they were in on the decision to snatch some beer. Everybody's real sorry and all and they've learned a valuable lesson."

"I'm not sure Woody and Tony will admit to anything except the beer. They have been pretty vocal in that they knew nothing about the robbery."

"That's where you come in, Rodney. That's what defense lawyers are for. You've got to convince them that all three must stick together and stick to one story. Trust me on this. I've been doing this for over thirty years and I'm very good at what I do. I know the judges and the prosecutors and they know me."

"Indeed they do."

"There's a way out of this for all three boys, Rodney. We just need to use a bit of creative storytelling, let each boy take a bite of the blame, and everybody gets out in one piece."

Rodney took a sip of coffee and a deep breath. Clifford Nance was very persuasive but Rodney really didn't appreciate being pressured by another lawyer. Not like this.

Rodney asked, "What makes you so sure you can convince Jack Hogan to reduce the armed robbery to a misdemeanor?"

Clifford offered a smug smile as if he knew everything. "Jack and I go way back. We've squared off in the courtroom many times. Murder trials, drug trials, you name it. We have great respect for each other, respect that has been earned. This is not a serious case, Rodney. This is the story of three boys out joyriding and doing something stupid. Again, nobody got hurt. I know Jack and I know I can convince him to back off and do Garth a favor. The Tuckers are nice people, unlike most of the criminal defendants Jack prosecutes. We just need for you to convince your clients to go along with our plan."

"It's not going to be easy."

"Do you really believe that Woody and Tony had no idea what Garth was up to?"

"I'm not so sure about that. I've always had my doubts about their stories."

"Now you're talking, Rodney. I have doubts, too. I would bet good money that those boys ran out of beer and talked about stealing some more. And I'll bet that the judge will think so, too."

"Okay, I'll talk to my clients. I'm sure this will take several conversations."

"Well, let's hurry along. I'd like to cut a deal with Hogan before the grand jury gets the case."

Nance smiled properly and stood. Conversation over. He walked Rodney to the door, paused, and rubbed his chin. "Say, Rodney, how long do you plan to work for Monk?"

"Oh, I don't know, a couple of years maybe."

"Then what?"

"I'd like to go into private practice, join a nice law firm, and specialize in criminal defense. I love the courtroom and can see a career there."

"That's what I did and I have no regrets. One day soon,

after this case is over, let's have a conversation about your future. I'm always looking for young talent. We have seven lawyers now and need at least two more."

"I would really enjoy that conversation, Mr. Nance."

"It's Clifford."

CHAPTER 21

On a cold, rainy afternoon, Theo was at his desk in his little office in the rear of Boone & Boone, and instead of doing his boring homework he was kicked back in his old hand-me-down swivel office chair watching the rain splatter against his window. Judge snored under his desk, inches from Theo's sneakers. At times the rain fell hard and the wind whistled against the roof. Then it slacked off and almost quit. He had been studying the rain and the wind for some time because his Geometry was particularly boring, they were suffering through polygons; and his Chemistry was quite dull, they were memorizing compounds; and, well, nothing at the moment offered any excitement. So he was doing what he often did at the age of thirteen—thinking about life and wondering what it would be like in a few short years when he was grown and driving and dealing with high school issues. He even had a thought or two about college, but couldn't imagine the day when he was forced to leave home and go out into the world without his parents and his dog. He had already done a bit of research online and had yet to find a college that allowed its freshmen to bring their dogs to school.

But that was a few years away. He had more pressing issues at hand. A book report for English. A speech for Government. The Major was watching him closely and monitoring his merit badge progress. The guy had practically set a deadline for Theo to become an Eagle Scout. April Finnemore's father had left home again, for the umpteenth time, and her mother was still crazy. Theo was afraid she, April, might just run away and vanish forever.

The hours passed and the sky grew darker and Theo kept daydreaming. A soft knock on the rear door startled him and brought him back to life. Woody barreled in, shaking off rainwater. He was soaked.

"Come in," Theo said.

"I'm in, Theo, and I'm freezing. Give me your coat."

Theo pulled his jacket off a wall hook and tossed it to Woody. "What in the world are you doing out on the streets in a rainstorm?"

"Well, I'm not here just because I miss you, I can promise you that," Woody said as he put on the coat. Judge was awake and sniffing around Woody's ankles. Woody glanced at the open door and asked, "Can we talk?"

"Sure." Theo got up, closed the door, and retook his seat. "This must be important."

"It is. Tony and I just spent an hour with Rodney Wall. The guy's a creep. He fed us this line about buying into Garth's story of the gun. Wall wants Tony and me to help cover Garth's butt by saying the gun belonged to me, that Tony knew about it, that we offered it to Garth so that he could get us some more beer, which we all wanted."

"Your lawyer wants you to lie?"

"Yes. He says that we need to go along with the story because Clifford Nance is tight with the prosecutor, what's his name—"

"Jack Hogan."

"Right, Hogan, and that if we all tell the same story and we all take some of the blame then we'll all get off light, including, of course, Garth."

"That's terrible, Woody. You had never seen the gun before."

"Tell me about it. The bad part is that Wall, our very own lawyer and the one we're stuck with because we can't afford another one, wants us to take the deal. He kept calling it a 'good deal.' He said Mr. Nance had pretty much worked out everything with Jack Hogan. We'll all get light sentences and Garth will avoid a felony conviction, which will stay on his record forever and ruin his life in every way possible. You should've been there, Theo. It was pathetic watching our lawyer try to convince us to take a deal and lie about everything."

"What did you say?"

"I said no. Tony said no. Wall got ticked off at us for saying no, said we'll have to go to trial and that Judge Pendergrast will probably not believe us because we're brothers and brothers tend to stick together. Wall said that. He also said that it was unlikely the judge would believe that we, Tony and me, knew nothing about what Garth was up to. The bottom line, Theo, is that our lawyer doesn't believe us and he wants to cut a deal to impress Mr. Bigshot Clifford Nance."

"I can't believe this."

"I know, I know. The guy is more concerned with taking care of Garth Tucker than us. We have to get another lawyer, Theo. Can you represent us? I know you're only thirteen but you'd do a better job than Wall."

"Sorry. Come back in about twelve years."

"What about your mother?"

"No. I had to twist her arm to do the bail hearing, and

she's convinced she did a lousy job there. She doesn't like criminal law and wants to stay away from it."

"Your dad?"

Theo snorted. "You'd probably get the death penalty. My dad hasn't seen a courtroom in decades."

"What about Ike?"

"No license, same as me. I have an idea. Let's talk to the Major, tell him everything. He's worked with Wall before and I'll bet he's not afraid to get in the guy's face."

Woody had stopped shivering, though water still dripped from his hair and ran down his cheeks. "I like it," he said softly. "You gotta do something, Theo."

"Did Wall say what would happen if you and Tony got convicted?"

"Yeah. That's the sick part. He said we would be sent to a juvenile prison for a long time. How scary is that, Theo? Our own lawyer trying to scare us with prison if we don't do what he says."

"What did you say?"

"Tony got mad, got real mad, and said if he was any good at being a lawyer then we wouldn't get convicted because we are innocent. They exchanged words, things got pretty ugly, and he told us to leave. We're at war with our own lawyer."

"Let's go find the Major."

They found him at home. On the phone he invited them over, and they rode their bikes through the rain. Luckily, he didn't live too far away. His home was a quaint bungalow in the center of town, an older house he and his wife had beautifully renovated when they retired to Strattenburg. The boys had been there before several times for scouting sessions and merit badge workshops.

Mrs. Ludwig gave them towels and served them hot cocoa, which had never tasted better. After she disappeared, Woody retold the story of his and Tony's disastrous meeting with their lawyer. As always, the Major listened carefully without comment until Woody finished.

"This is disturbing," he said.

Theo, ever ready to join the conversation, asked, "If Woody tells this new story, isn't that perjury?"

The Major replied, "Of course it is. A false statement made under oath in court is perjury, which is another crime. It will only make matters worse, Woody. There's no way you can take the stand and tell this story."

"Oh, I'm not going to," Woody said.

"What about Tony?" the Major asked.

"We're sticking together and we're sticking to the truth. It's that simple. We don't care what happens to Garth. He's got his own lawyer and his family has some money."

The Major rubbed his chin, deep in thought. He was frowning and not pleased with what he was hearing. Theo interrupted things with, "Shouldn't you report this to the judge, Major, tell him that this lawyer is trying to get his clients to lie in court?"

"Maybe, but not right now. Let's see how things play out. Your trial is a week from Wednesday so we have some time. Perhaps I'll meet with Rodney Wall and explain things to him, let him know that you and Tony are not going along with this new story."

Woody said, "Okay, but here's what's bugging me. Wall says that our story, the true story, is not that believable. Three teenagers in a car drinking beer and needing some more. The plan to rob a place for more beer and a little cash to boot. And two of the three know nothing of the plan? I kind of see his point. Maybe that is too hard to believe. Then, the two guys who claim to be innocent are also brothers, who, of course, can be expected to say anything to cover for each other. Maybe our case is not as strong as we think."

"I agree," said Theo, though no one asked his opinion. "So the big question is: What if you go to trial and the judge finds you guilty?"

"Exactly," Woody said. "What if we're found guilty and sent away for a year or two? That would be the end of the world. Just go ahead and shoot me."

The Major said, "Let's not overreact here. I'll meet with Mr. Wall as soon as possible and let's see how that goes."

"I have a question," Theo said. "If Woody and Tony decide to go along with the plan here and take some of the blame, what crime will they plead guilty to? I don't understand."

The Major smiled and said, "Well, fortunately or unfortunately, there is no shortage of crimes on the books. I can see a deal where they would plead guilty to a misdemeanor like malicious mischief or disorderly conduct, something like that. A lesser offense that would not lead to jail time and be removed from their records after they turn eighteen."

Theo looked at Woody and asked, "Could you do that, Woody? Could you plead guilty if it meant no jail time for all three of you?"

Woody gritted his teeth and said, "No way. I'm not guilty."

Major Ludwig smiled and nodded his approval.

CHAPTER 22

It was a slow night at Santo's and Tony had only four pizzas to deliver. He was alone. Daisy discouraged Woody from any more pizza runs, and Tony did not offer. Woody was at home, supposedly doing his homework. Daisy was pulling a late shift at the restaurant. Their stepfather had not been home in weeks, as if he was avoiding all the drama.

The first delivery was to a student duplex near Stratten College, a street Tony knew well. He carried a pepperoni supreme to the front door, knocked and waited. It was the typical overcrowded student place with bikes chained to the front railings and empty beer cans scattered through the neglected flower beds. The door opened and a pretty coed asked him to step inside. He did so, handed her the pizza, and waited as she fetched the money. A college boy walked through the den and said hello. Tony waited, part of the routine of delivering pizza.

From the back hallway, Garth Tucker appeared and said, "Hey, Tony, what's up?"

"Not much. What are you doing here?" Tony was surprised to see him but not startled. Seniors at Strattenburg High were known to visit friends at the college. Still, bumping into him on a pizza run on a random weeknight was too much of a coincidence.

"Friends of mine. I hang out here sometimes." The two saw each other at school occasionally but rarely spoke. Since their arrests, they had tried to avoid each other. Tony especially wanted nothing to do with Garth. The girl returned to the den and handed Tony a twenty. He pulled change out of his pocket and gave it to her.

Garth said, "Say, Tony, you got a minute? I need to discuss something with you."

"What's there to discuss? And I have three more pizzas to deliver."

"There's a small patio out back. Just the two of us. Won't take but a minute."

Tony looked around and didn't like the setting. He heard other male voices in the rear of the apartment. The girl was gone, as was the pizza. "What's on your mind?"

"It's private, Tony. Let's step outside."

Tony could handle Garth in a fistfight, but he wasn't sure how many others might decide to join in. Cautiously, he followed Garth into the kitchen, where he saw no one, and through the rear door onto a brick patio. A dim yellow bulb provided the only light. Tony looked around to make sure it wasn't an ambush. Garth seemed nervous but sincere.

He said, "Look, first things first. I did a dumb thing and got us all busted. My bad. I was drunk and pulled a boneheaded move. But I'm not drinking now. I've quit and I'm behaving myself. I'm still in trouble, though, and I need some help. My lawyer says you guys don't want to play along with our line of defense. I wish you would. It would help me tremendously."

"We're not lying in court, Garth, if that's what you're asking. You know perfectly well what happened and you're just trying to change the facts. Sorry."

"Okay, okay. I'm not here to argue, Tony, that's not going to help us. There's a way out of this mess if we can all stick together."

"You mean there's a way out for you. Pin the blame on us, or especially on Woody because he's thirteen, and you get to walk. We're not stupid, Garth. You may have a bigshot lawyer, but it's obvious what's going on. The answer is no. We are not walking into a courtroom and lying. That will only make matters worse."

Garth kept his cool and showed no signs of anger. No one else appeared in the kitchen. As the minutes passed, the situation looked less and less like an ambush. "Do you realize what a felony conviction does to me, Tony? It means I'll go to jail, maybe for years, and my life is ruined. No college, no career, no nothing. Why can't you guys help me here?"

"Because we're innocent and you're not. That simple."

"Simple. Here's what's simple." Garth reached into an inside pocket of his jacket, and for a second Tony's heart skipped a beat. Then he whipped out an envelope and said, "This is five thousand dollars cash, Tony. All yours. Just go with our story and keep the money. Think of how much your family could use this money."

Tony was stunned and took a step back. Garth pressed ahead. "Come on, Tony. It's cash, cannot be traced, and it's all yours. Yours and Woody's. You can do with it whatever you want. Just agree to stick to our little story and help me out. The money is yours."

Tony had never known anyone with $5,000 cash in their pockets, especially a high school student. He stared at the envelope, shook his head in disbelief, and said, "You gotta be kidding."

"Do you really think I'm kidding here, Tony. My future is on the line and I need your help. You need the money, I need a favor."

Tony took another step back and said, "Okay, okay, let me think about this. If Woody and I play along, then we admit to some of the guilt. That means we could go back to jail, right?"

"You're headed back to jail anyway because you busted probation with the drinking, at least according to my lawyer."

"Maybe, but that's no big deal, according to my lawyer." Tony was certain that Garth's lawyer was far more experienced than Rodney Wall, but Wall was all he had.

Garth smiled and tried to seem relaxed. Just a couple of old pals. "Look, Tony, let's not argue, okay? You're right, I'm wrong. But there's a way out for everybody here. Maybe you get a weekend in jail, maybe the same for Woody, but nothing serious. And you've got a pocket full of cash to ease the pain."

"Bribing a witness sounds like a pretty serious crime to me."

Garth returned the envelope to his pocket and said, "I know nothing about a bribe. Just think about it, Tony. We've got a few days, but not many."

"I need to deliver some pizzas."

CHAPTER 23

The Stratten County Grand Jury met twice a month in the main courtroom to review serious criminal charges. There were eighteen members, all registered voters of the county and all serving six month terms. The grand jury was controlled by Jack Hogan, who presented the cases. Like most grand juries, it almost always did whatever the chief prosecutor wanted. The majority of the cases were slam dunks. The defendants were guilty, and there were plenty of witnesses to prove it.

Unfortunately, each session was busy, each docket was long—there was no shortage of crime in Stratten County. Mr. Hogan presented each case, gave a summary of the facts, occasionally presented a witness or two, and then asked the grand jury to vote to indict the accused. The indictment was the formal charge of wrongdoing.

Drug cases consumed eighty percent of the docket, and after half an hour the grand jurors were usually bored with their work.

The grand jury convened at three p.m. on a Thursday afternoon, an hour after Judge Gantry had finished with some motion hearings. The courtroom was cleared and a deputy made sure the proceedings were private.

Jack Hogan was planning to present the armed robbery case against Garth Tucker. Clem Hamm was waiting to testify for the State. At the last minute, though, Clifford Nance convinced Hogan to delay the case until the following month. Nance assured the prosecutor that he was working on a deal with the three defendants that would be agreeable with everyone. Hogan didn't really care. He had more serious matters to worry about than an eighteen-year-old kid goofing around with a water pistol.

The case of State versus Garth Tucker was postponed until further notice.

The other case was not. It was officially titled: "In The Matter of Tony and Woodrow Lambert," and it was set for trial in Youth Court first thing on a Wednesday morning. All necessary parties were summoned, with the exception of Mr. Theodore Boone, who had no role in the case and was banished to his labors at Strattenburg Middle School.

The afternoon before, Theo swung by Ike's office for an urgent meeting. He called ahead of time, explained to his uncle that things were serious, and told the story. Ike listened intently and found it hard to believe that an eighteen-year-old defendant was offering a cash bribe to a potential witness.

"They cannot take that money!" Ike said. "I don't care how big the bribe, those boys cannot take the money."

"They're thinking about it," Theo said. "At first they said no way, but then they started thinking about what they could do with the money, how it would help the family and take pressure off their mom, all that stuff."

"Nonsense, Theo. Here's a likely scenario. Let's say Garth has the cash and Tony agrees to accept it on the sly. What if some of the bills are marked? What if Garth is wearing a wire? What if there's a camera watching everything? Well, then, Tony gets compromised. Garth can't run to the police and point a finger at Tony because Garth is just as guilty, even guiltier, but he's got some real leverage over Tony. This could be a trap, Theo. It's a bad deal because Garth is trying to bribe Tony into lying, and it's a rotten deal because Garth might be trying to set up Tony. You tell Woody that this is a no-brainer."

"I thought so. But I'm worried about them. Woody is really upset by this."

"Tell Woody to trust his gut and say no. Nothing good will happen. Does their mother know about the bribe?"

"No, I don't think so. Woody says I'm the only other person who knows about it. Should I tell Mom and Dad?"

Ike sipped his beer and scratched his nose. "No. You know how uptight they are. They're officers of the court and ethically bound to report wrongdoing, especially crimes involving the wheels of justice. If they knew one witness was trying to bribe another, they'd probably freak out and run to the judge. Let's leave them out of it for now."

"I agree. They would only complicate matters. Should I tell Judge Gantry? He and I are pretty tight."

"Right now I say no, but let me think about it."

They thought about it for a long time, the only sound was Bob Dylan singing softly about lost love. Finally, Theo asked, "Where would Garth get five thousand dollars in cash?"

"Who knows? I doubt if it's his. I doubt if Clifford Nance knows anything about it. He's an ethical lawyer. So, the money is probably coming from Garth's family. His father is a high roller who borrows a lot and takes big risks. Maybe he figures five thousand bucks is nothing to keep his kid out of prison. Who knows? The important thing is for your friends to run away from this kid and his cash. Tell them to go to court, tell the truth, and deal with whatever happens."

"I've told Woody that, more than once."

"This is troubling, Theo. And it's dangerous."

"Does this stuff happen all the time, Ike? I mean, you know how much I love trials and courtrooms and how much I respect the law, and it's never occurred to me that the witness on the stand might be lying because he took a bribe."

"I don't know, Theo. I wasn't much of a courtroom lawyer. Plus, I got chewed up by the system so I'm probably not the one to ask. But, no, I don't believe this stuff happens all the time. This is pretty wild. An eighteen-year-old kid offering cash."

"Kinda makes me sick."

Unknown to Theo, Woody was at the same time having a similar conversation not far away in the den of Major Ludwig's bungalow. Not surprisingly, the Major's reaction was similar to Ike's. He was shocked at the idea of a bribe and adamant that Woody and Tony stay away from it.

"Did Tony actually see the money, the cash?" the Major asked.

"No, it was in a white envelope. He pulled it out of the pocket of his jacket."

"So, I suppose this could be a bluff."

"Maybe," Woody said, thoroughly bewildered. "I don't know what to think or what to do. Tony has talked of nothing else but taking the money and using it to help Mom."

"You, Tony, and your mom are going to survive, one way or the other, and without taking a bribe from Garth. We know he's not a very bright kid and this is further proof. Trying to bribe a witness is a really dumb idea. Nothing good can happen."

"I agree. I'm just worried about Tony."

"I'll talk to Tony before the trial starts and make things real clear. You guys are sticking to the truth, right, Woody?"

"Yes, sir."

CHAPTER 24

An additional bailiff stood outside the courtroom door to keep away the curious and uninvolved. Judge Pendergrast wanted complete privacy during the trial. It would not last long and there was nothing else on his docket for the day.

The Lambert boys sat at the defense table with their lawyer between them. Their relationship was still tense. As recently as yesterday Rodney Wall had tried to convince them again that they should go along with the Clifford Nance story and take some of the blame. But Woody and Tony were tired of Wall and his lack of decisiveness. He did not know about the bribe. They were certainly not telling anyone else. They knew the truth and they knew far more than their lawyer; thus, they had little respect for him.

Daisy sat in the front row close behind them. She really needed Theo to lean on, but poor Theo was suffering through Spanish and was perfectly miserable. Major Ludwig sat beside her, arms crossed over his chest.

A few feet away, the Youth Court prosecutor, Ms. Bagdell, shuffled her papers and waited to begin. She would go first and she seemed a bit too nervous.

When Judge Pendergrast finished reading a page he peered out over his reading glasses and said, "This matter involves some serious charges against Tony and Woody Lambert. I believe I know most of the facts so I don't need to hear opening statements. Ms. Bagdell, please call your first witness."

"Mr. Clem Hamm," Ms. Bagdell said, sitting. In Youth Court, it was not necessary to stand to address the judge or the witnesses.

Clem Hamm hurried in and was sworn to tell the truth. Judge Pendergrast had reviewed his testimony from Garth's preliminary hearing, and knew every detail that he repeated. On cross-examination, Rodney Wall made sure that it was clear that neither Clem nor any of the store's surveillance cameras ever caught sight of the Lambert boys.

When Clem stepped down, Ms. Bagdell offered to call

a witness who would play the surveillance tapes from the robbery, but Judge Pendergrast declined. He surprised everyone when he said, "I've already reviewed them. They reveal nothing involving these two juveniles." Thirty minutes into the trial, it was apparent that His Honor had studied the case carefully and knew as much as anyone. This was not unusual.

The next witness was a police officer who described the arrests of the three shortly after they left Kall's Grocery. He found neither weapons nor cash on the Lambert boys. Garth had cash in one pocket and the pistol in the other. The pistol was produced, introduced into evidence, handled by the witness and the judge, and put away. Judge Pendergrast took endless notes but seemed as though he'd heard it all before.

The next witness was another policeman who planned to testify about the Breathalyzer results. Rodney Wall, though, interrupted matters and said his clients had already agreed to admit that they had been drinking beer.

Judge Pendergrast said, "I have the reports. Woody Lambert registered point zero six. Same for Tony. This is correct?"

"It is," Wall said, and the witness was excused. The trial was moving at a dizzying pace.

The next witness was the big one. Ms. Bagdell called Garth Tucker to the stand. A bailiff fetched him from the hallway, and when Garth walked into the courtroom Clifford Nance was with him.

For the occasion, Garth wore a dark suit and tie and his new haircut was even shorter. He tried to play the cool game and act as though this was all routine, but he was nervous. He swore to tell the truth, took his seat, refused to make eye contact with either Woody or Tony, and looked at Clifford Nance seated in the back row, not far away.

After a few preliminary questions, Ms. Bagdell asked, "On the night in question, where did you meet Tony and Woody?"

"I was buying gas at the Shell station on Cooper Extended."

"And why did they get into your car?"

"I don't know. Tony and I talked and decided to go cruising. I had some beer. The little kid just sort of tagged along."

"And the three of you drove around drinking beer?"

"Yes."

"How much did you drink?"

Judge Pendergrast said abruptly, "His blood alcohol content was point twelve. Beyond legally drunk. I have the report here, Ms. Bagdell, please move along."

"Uh, yes, sir," she said awkwardly as she reached for another sheet of paper. "Okay, so why did you decide to stop at Kall's Grocery?"

Garth took a deep breath, looked long and hard at Clifford Nance, and said, as if perfectly rehearsed, "I decline to answer that question under the rights afforded me by the Fifth Amendment."

Ms. Bagdell looked at Judge Pendergrast, who looked at the witness and asked, "So, you are refusing to incriminate yourself?"

"Yes, sir."

"Very well. Please note that this witness's attorney, Mr. Clifford Nance, is in the courtroom. Proceed, Ms. Bagdell."

She asked, "You guys were drinking beer. Did you need more? Did you go to Kall's because you needed more?"

"I plead the Fifth Amendment."

"Did you buy any gas at Kall's?"

"No."

"Whose idea was it to go to Kall's?"

"I plead the Fifth Amendment."

"Did you have a pistol of any type with you when you drove to the store?"

"I plead the Fifth Amendment."

"Did you take a pistol into the store?"

"I plead the Fifth Amendment."

Ms. Bagdell lifted the pistol from a table and showed it to the witness. "Did you purchase this?"

"I plead the Fifth Amendment."

She threw up her hands and looked at the bench. Judge Pendergrast was obviously irritated and leaned over to the witness. "I assume, son, that you have no plans to answer any more questions about what happened that night, correct?"

Garth offered a sappy smile and said, "That's right, Judge. Upon the advice of my lawyer, I'm not answering any more questions."

Judge Pendergrast looked at Clifford Nance, who was nodding his agreement.

"Very well, the witness is excused."

Garth strutted to the rear of the courtroom where he and his lawyer took seats on the rear bench. Clifford Nance wanted to hear every word uttered by the Lambert boys.

Tony went first and told the same story he had been repeating since that fateful night. Rodney Wall did a good job of walking him through it, step by careful step, with nothing left out. Judge Pendergrast asked a number of questions, as he was prone to do, and once again let everybody know that he had full command of the facts. His preparation was impressive.

On cross-examination, Ms. Bagdell blundered. Veteran trial lawyers know that you never ask a question if you don't already know the answer. She, evidently, had not learned this.

She asked Tony, "Have you ever been in Garth's car before?"

"Never."

"Have you ever been to Kall's Grocery before?"

"Never."

"Had you ever seen the pistol before?"

"Never."

In a matter of seconds, she took away any suspicion that Tony had been involved in the planning of the robbery.

She quickly wrapped up her cross-examination.

Woody took the stand. He was nervous, especially with Garth and Clifford Nance staring at him, but he was determined to be a good witness. He looked at Major Ludwig, who gave him a firm nod of the head, and he launched into his story. It was the same as Tony's, the same as before, with no variations at all. The more he testified the more confident he became, and about halfway through he wished Theo could be there to hear it all.

Like Tony, he placed all blame on Garth, and managed to stare him down as he did so. It was a wonderful moment. Garth, the cocky kid with a muscle car and cute girl and wealthy family and a wild side that was crashing in on him as he sat there protected by the best lawyer money could buy, but he wasn't so cool right now. He looked worried because he knew the truth was against him, and he couldn't change it. He couldn't shift some of the blame to other people.

"Any cross, Ms. Bagdell?" Judge Pendergrast asked.

"I don't think so." She had nothing to work with and she wasn't about to ask any more half-baked questions.

"Any more witnesses, Mr. Wall?"

"Well, Your Honor, I was going to call Daisy Lambert, the mother, but it seems as though the Court has probably heard enough this morning."

"Indeed the Court has. But I'm not going to prevent you from calling your witnesses."

"I think we're finished here, Judge," Wall said wisely.

Without a moment's hesitation, Judge Pendergrast launched into his ruling. "I find both Tony and Woody Lambert to be credible witnesses. And though I am usually suspicious of identical testimony offered by siblings or close friends, I am not suspicious today. Their narratives are plausible, reasonable, believable, and the Court has no reason to doubt them. Indeed, there is absolutely no testimony to the contrary. They are charged with being accomplices, which means they supposedly knew something of the crime, armed robbery, before it took place. The evidence is to the contrary. The only witness who could possibly implicate the Lambert brothers is obviously Garth Tucker, and he chose not to do so. For reasons known only to himself and his very experienced lawyer, Mr. Tucker chose to plead the Fifth Amendment. That is his right, but it leaves nothing for the prosecution to pursue.

"Therefore, I find Tony and Woody Lambert not guilty of the crimes of being accomplices to armed robbery. For Woody, I will deal with the underage drinking matter another day. Same for Tony, but he also has the sticky issue of a probation violation. He can certainly expect a few more nights in detention. But we'll handle that another day. For now, both juveniles are free to go. The bond for Tony will be extinguished. The restrictions for both are hereby terminated. Woody, you are free to leave the county and go camping anywhere you want."

CHAPTER 25

Outside the courthouse, near the statue of General Stratten, they stopped to catch a breath. Rodney Wall was smiling ear to ear as though he had just pulled off a major victory and wanted everyone to slap him on the back. No one did. Woody and Tony were sick of the guy. Daisy didn't trust him. Major Ludwig held him in low esteem.

"Congratulations," Rodney said, and then waited for someone to congratulate him.

"When do we go back to court?" Daisy asked. "On the drinking charges?"

"I'll check with the judge, let you know, but it's nothing to worry about."

They nodded, said nothing, and Rodney finally took a hint. "Well, gotta run now. Got some new clients down at the jail." No one said good-bye. They watched him walk away, and before Tony could say something unpleasant about him, the Major said, "I guess you two should hustle back to school."

Woody and Tony nodded. These days they were terrified about missing class.

The Major said, "I'm starving. Pappy's should be cleared out by now. My treat."

Pappy's Deli was a legendary downtown hole-in-the-wall that was famous for its pastrami subs and onion rings, and both boys jumped at the chance. The four of them took off down Main Street, walking briskly and chatting about the trial. They were innocent! No more worries about being shipped off to a juvenile detention center, no more fears about the future. They had stuck to the truth, testified to it faithfully, and Judge Pendergrast believed them.

Daisy said less than the others. As their mother, she was overjoyed almost to the point of tears. Her boys would no longer be treated like criminals. Both seemed determined to stay out of trouble. Perhaps she could sleep now. Perhaps her life was finally taking a turn for the better.

Theo was suffering through another boring study hall with Mr. Mount. He was going through the motions of doing homework but his mind was elsewhere. He firmly believed that he had the right to be in Youth Court that morning to witness the trial, and to provide assistance if necessary. After all, he knew as much about the case as anyone. He had led the charge to free Woody and Tony from jail. He had advised Woody along the way. He had coached him with his testimony. He had provided crucial advice, especially about the bribe. He knew far more about the case than Woody's lawyer.

However, none of that mattered. There he was, staring at Spanish verbs and thinking of nothing but the proceedings before Judge Pendergrast. He had a large knot in his stomach that made it hard to concentrate. What if Woody and Tony were found guilty? What if Judge Pendergrast didn't believe them but instead found Garth to be a more credible witness? What if Woody got sentenced to some dreadful juvenile prison?

His cell phone vibrated. Normally, all cell phones were confiscated by Mr. Mount at the beginning of each class and placed in a cardboard box on his desk. But because of the trial, Theo had been allowed to keep his just in case there was news.

There was! Woody texted: Trial over. Lambert boys not guilty! Not guilty!!! Free at last!!

"All right!" Theo blurted as he jumped to his feet.

"What is it, Theo?" Mr. Mount asked as the entire class jolted to attention.

They turned onto a narrow side street and arrived at Pappy's minutes before two p.m. They found a table in the corner, placed their orders, sipped colas and iced tea as they waited and talked.

"How serious is my little probation thing?" Tony asked the Major.

"Serious. You heard the judge all but promise more jail time, but it might be something we can work around."

"I don't understand," Daisy said.

"Well, jail would mean absence from school. Right now Tony's in class and his grades are improving. We should delay the hearing and give both of you time to show perfect attendance in school and a big improvement in grades. Both of you. Get the grades up. Get a couple of letters from your teachers, and I can go to the judge and lean on him."

"You've done this before?" Daisy asked.

"Yes, it's my role as a Youth Court volunteer. Judge

Pendergrast is rather old-fashioned and places great emphasis on education. Show him you're serious about school and he'll cut you some slack. He'll also want random drug tests for the next year."

"For both of us?" Woody asked.

"Sure. Why not? You're not messing with anything, right?"

"Right, but I just don't want to get embarrassed by some random drug test."

"You won't be embarrassed. It's routine and you'll have no choice."

"They can do it," Daisy said firmly.

Their lunch arrived and the small table was quickly covered with large platters of thick subs and piles of hot onion rings, enough food for ten. Daisy worried too much to eat. Major Ludwig was an old soldier with iron discipline and refused to gain an ounce. Woody and Tony, though, were teenage boys, and they attacked the food like starving refugees.

After a few silent moments of serious eating, Daisy asked the Major, "So what happens next with Garth?"

"Oh, I have no idea. That's another matter in another court."

"Will Woody and Tony be forced to testify in his trial?" she asked.

The Major wiped his mouth with a paper napkin, shrugged, and said, "I would think so, if his case goes all the way to a jury trial."

"Do you think it will?" Tony asked.

"I have no inside knowledge, but I doubt that Garth will ever face a jury. He's dead guilty and he can't lie his way out of it. There are three eyewitnesses—the two of you, and the guy in the store. Plus the surveillance cameras. I suspect Clifford Nance will figure out a way to keep him away from a jury and out of jail."

"How can he possibly avoid jail?" Daisy asked.

The Major shrugged again. "His family has money. He has the best lawyer. It's his first offense. Nobody got hurt. I hate to say it, Daisy, but there are different rules for different people. It's not fair, but it's the way the system goes."

And, thought Woody and Tony, he has a pocket full of cash to bribe someone else.

"Let's worry about Garth later," the Major said. "Today is a great day for the Lambert family, so let's savor the win."

"Great idea," Tony said.

Theo called an emergency session for four p.m. at Guff's Frozen Yogurt on Main Street. He arrived early, talked to the owner, and got two long tables in the rear. They filled quickly as almost all of Mr. Mount's homeroom arrived. Mr. Mount himself walked in at four on the dot and ordered a double caramel fudge.

When Woody strolled in, alone, he set off a small roar as his friends welcomed him and gave him the seat of honor. After a round of high fives and fist pumps and even a hug or two, Woody attacked a coconut cream as Theo called for order.

He held his hands out dramatically and said, "Once again, my fellow Americans, justice has prevailed. The innocent have been set free. The wheels of justice have produced the right verdict."

"Blah, blah, blah," Chase added and got a laugh.

Theo pretended to ignore him. "Woody, congratulations. Now, all of us are dying to hear what happened in court. And start at the beginning."

Woody took a big bite of frozen yogurt, savored the attention, and said, "Well, I was never that worried."